Curved Light

Curved Light

ALAN WALL

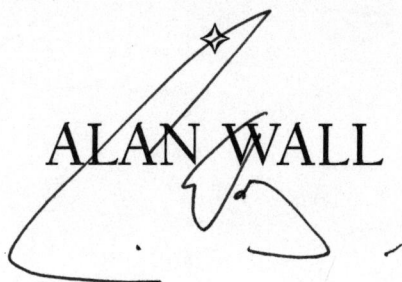

BELLEW PUBLISHING ✦ LONDON

First published in Great Britain in 1994 by
Bellew Publishing Company Limited
8 Balham Hill, London SW12 9EA

ISBN 1 85725 101 6

Typeset in the UK by Antony Gray
Printed and bound in Great Britain by
Hartnolls Ltd, Bodmin, Cornwall

Contents

One Night Before the War: 1914

It was a warm summer evening when Aubrey Innis left Buckingham Palace. A cab rattled towards him but he ignored it and
started walking swiftly up Constitution Hill. He was followed by
a young woman wearing a white muslin dress and a straw hat.
Over her shoulder hung a large black leather bag.

The papers in his hand did not in fact contain the orders of
state his pursuer imagined. They were simply notes for his book,
Those Who Command. He had gone that day, or so he thought,
to interview His Majesty, for one of his chapters was devoted to
King George. He had not however met the monarch himself.
Instead he was given an audience with his private secretary,
Lord Stamfordham, a man grave in carriage yet affable in
demeanour, who had been instructed to provide the young man
with all the information it might be proper for him to receive.

Aubrey's pace grew even more rapid as he considered some of
Stamfordham's remarks. Suffragettes. Ireland. Trades union
militants. The King's private secretary, cultivated far beyond the
requirements of his post, quoted Milton:

> ' . . . disastrous twilight sheds
> On half the nations, and with fear of change
> Perplexes monarchs.'

His Majesty, Stamfordham had explained, was a man imprisoned in a constitution. Innis came to a halt to consider that. He
was within sight of Apsley House by now. I don't suppose I'd
have got an interview with the Iron Duke either, he thought to
himself. He spun round suddenly and kicked a pebble at the
palace wall. The young woman ten paces behind him froze. She

reached hurriedly into her bag and rummaged there as though searching for something momentarily misplaced. Her fingers felt only the cold steel of the handcuffs. Innis noticed her. Pretty, he thought. Bony but pretty, her face half hidden under her hat. Then off he went again.

She had to shuffle and skip along behind him, clutching now her hat and now her leather bag. She'd waited down there till a likely one came out. The minute she saw him through the iron railings she knew this was one of them. His stride announced that he was strolling into the century he would inherit. She was the daughter of King's Counsel, Alfred Merrill, who had come to represent for her the source of all constriction and restraint. And some filament connected her father to that palace. So this younger echo of him who sliced the air ahead of her had to be connected too, for which reason she would follow him back to his lair and discover what she could never fathom from her father: from whence they derived their power.

The policemen eyed her casually as they ambled down the hill. And once again she saw that smile they passed between them like a masonic riddle. He stopped suddenly in front of her and kicked a stone, talking merrily to himself at the same time as he turned and stared at her as though she had no right to be there at all. Just reminding himself he owns the world, she thought, so why not kick it, stare through it, lecture the evening breeze?

Through Knightsbridge they went, past Harrods to the left and the Oratory to the right until, at the eastern edges of the Natural History Museum, Aubrey Innis pressed the bell of Number Eight, Cromwell Place, South Kensington. As he was ushered inside, Claire Merrill turned the corner in time to see him disappear. She leaned against the wall a full two minutes until she could breathe again without an effort.

Aubrey had been shown upstairs into the presence of his old friend Arthur Smithson-Lowe – of some fame in London, if not exactly notoriety. The art-dealer marvelled at Aubrey's fluidity of movement as he entered the room. Sinuous charmer.

'Champagne?' he asked, already pouring. 'How was His Majesty?'

Innis sank most of his drink before replying.

'I didn't . . . actually see the King himself.'

'Didn't actually see the King himself, Aubrey? I had thought that was the whole point of the exercise. Who *did* you see then?'

'Lord Stamfordham, his private secretary.'

'But I thought you said your father had arranged . . . '

'I know what I said Arthur. Anyway, there was evidently a misunderstanding of some sort . . . '

'But now this has happened with the King, with Northcliffe, with Asquith . . . '

'Any more of this?' Aubrey said abruptly, holding his glass out while turning away from his host's face. Smithson-Lowe re-filled his young friend's glass for him. He often walked about with a bottle in his hand – to the silent dismay of his servants – for he liked to discover the extent of his guests' appetites.

'Thirsty work evidently Aubrey – interviewing those who almost command.'

Aubrey Innis said nothing but walked over to the window. Across the road he noticed the unmistakeable features of the young lady who had followed him up Constitution Hill.

'I think I'm being tracked Arthur' he said, glad for an opportunity to change the subject.

Smithson-Lowe came over to the window and looked down.

'Some fellows might envy you that particular pursuit, Aubrey, by the look of her. Though she does have a hint of the suffragette about her. Beware. Another post box went up in flames today. It's getting so that one thinks twice before writing a letter. And I do worry a little for the gallery. After all, if they're prepared to carve up the Rokeby Venus, what price my Rovidas and Modiglianis? What was it the woman with the meat-cleaver said? They were out to destroy the myth of womanhood. Something like that anyway.'

Aubrey looked at the feast being spread.

'Who's coming?' he asked.

'Well now let me think, Aubrey. There's Marianne Morris, my assistant from the gallery, whom you've met. There's Orage, the socialist fellow who detests me but likes looking at my pictures. There's Nathan Corinth, the American writer – now you and he really should hit it off' he said with a smile. The bell rang again announcing Marianne Morris, fresh from the gallery on Cork Street.

One of the guests whom Smithson-Lowe had enumerated was a little delayed. Orage, the editor of *The New Age*, had received that afternoon a young man named Daniel Miskin. Daniel had first met Orage in Leeds when he was a schoolboy, and the editor one of the leading left-wing intellectuals of that serious northern town. Now Daniel lived and worked in London as an engineer and had become a Marxist. He had written his first article, *The Bourgeois Order and the Uses of Technology*, and submitted it in person to Orage. The editor, with all the subtlety at his disposal, had rejected it with much kindness and obliquity. In the process of explaining to Daniel that one had always to try to write, difficult though it was, as though one person at least might actually be reading, Orage had closed up his office and made his way to a tram. He found himself approaching South Kensington with Daniel still at his side. Well, why not? he thought.

'Daniel, come with me for something to eat at Arthur Smithson-Lowe's.'

Daniel demurred. After all, how could he? He was not dressed for such an occasion, had indeed never been dressed for such an occasion in the whole of his life. In any case he detested the bourgeoisie.

'Too late' Orage said, pulling his young companion from the tram. 'We're already here and both hungry as savages. You may observe one of the oppressors of the proletariat at closer quarters.'

Many were dressing or being dressed for dinner, as was King George the Fifth himself. No mirrors. Mirrors were for shaving only and the King had grown a beard. He was, after all, a sailor. In any case this ritual needed no reflection, having been perfected over half a lifetime of exact repetition. Though the King's features grew a little more mournful with each passing year, as he witnessed the goings-on of the people over whom he ruled. And even worse, the goings-on of those ruled over by others.

Daniel Miskin had not of course dressed for dinner because he had not expected to be given any – and certainly not the elaborate buffet now awaiting consumption in the house of Arthur Smithson-Lowe. As he stood beneath the white stucco portico of the doorway, he looked down at his shoes which were brown and unpolished, and at his hands, lined with ingrained oil and starting to sweat. Orage stood beside him, oblivious and whistling. The servant who appeared before them took them into the hallway and left them there a moment while he checked with his master. They were not gentlemen, that much he had seen at a glance. Arthur Smithson-Lowe appeared on his staircase, glass in hand.

'Ah, Orage, my dear fellow. And who is this? What special surprise have you brought me this time?'

'A friend of mine from Leeds' Orage said, 'about to become a contributor to *The Age*.'

They joined their host at the top of the stairs and as Miskin started to stare with disbelief at the treasures on plinths, on tables and on walls, Smithson-Lowe announced to the room:

'The hyperboreans have arrived. Two of them.' Miskin looked to Orage for clarification.

'Creatures from the extreme north' the editor said with a smile. 'Actually, Arthur, Leeds isn't in the *extreme* north, you know. There are places beyond it.'

'Well it seems extreme enough to me' came the reply. 'Anywhere north of Venice creeps towards the Arctic, in my book. The Renaissance did rather peter out the further upwards it went.'

The doorbell rang once more and the door opened to the clamour of a transatlantic voice:

'Where is he? WHERE IS HE?'

The rest of the guests fell silent as this new presence made its way up the stairs and into the room. The man who thus announced himself was holding a sheaf of photographs. He marched up to Arthur Smithson-Lowe, shook them in his face and shouted, 'Cretin!' Then he sat down in one of his host's large and comfortable chairs and closed his eyes. Arthur Smithson-Lowe looked down on him with a smile more of affection than contempt and announced, half to himself, 'Mr Nathan Corinth. Writer.'

Corinth was six feet tall with black curly hair that reached his shoulders. He had a nose like a blade and blue eyes that seemed curiously sunken in their sockets. He was dressed in a shabby opera cape and his grey fedora was still planted firmly on his head. Smithson-Lowe placed a gentle hand on his shoulder.

'You may undress, Nathan. Take off your hat and your cape. Drink my wines, eat my food. Explain to me, my dear, the cause of your wrath.'

Nathan was given a drink and disrobed of his more spectacular garments. And he started to speak. Barely audible at first, his voice increased in volume as his speech increased in passion. By the end of it he was pacing the substantial proportions of the room.

'I told you, Lowe, to go and see the Gaudiers. This house of yours is filled with second-rate paintings from the Renaissance. Someone had to pay the painter's wages. And now there is a new Renaissance – on however small a scale – and you will not lift a finger to help it. You cannot, surely, deny Gaudier's genius?'

'I deny no man's genius, Nathan' Smithson-Lowe said equably. 'In case you have missed it I have been promoting the work of

Lucio Rovida at considerable personal expense. Is he not a part of this new Renaissance?'

Corinth ignored this last remark, as he ignored all remarks that ran counter to his present theme.

'He lives in a railway arch with some foreign woman who's barking mad and he's very nearly starving to death. And he produces *these*.' Corinth raised the sheaf he had arrived with and waved them above his head. 'I have listened to your disquisitions on the fog of late Victoriana and how much you detest it. Here it has been overcome with the instinctive precision of a master. Just look at these. *Look* at them . . . '

Nathan Corinth fell into his own revery, staring at the photographs he held. The others stared at him in silence.

'Lowe' he shouted as his meditation ended, 'if you *won't* buy any of Gaudier's work, what on earth are you *for*?'

Serving men who spoke amongst themselves only in whispers gestured eloquently towards the banquet at the guests' disposal. Daniel Miskin, though fascinated by Corinth's disquisition, found the spread before him even more hypnotically dazzling. Everything appeared entwined with something else. Diminutive sausages carried spirals of segmented orange. Cheeses in more varieties than he even knew existed were garnished with cresses and pepper filaments and slivers of grape. There were eight different patés. Cold meats from he knew not which animals, sliced with preternatural precision and refinement. And he was now taking his first close-up look at caviare.

'Don't look at it, my dear fellow, eat it. You have come here from the North Pole. You must be distinctly peckish by now.'

The voice was Arthur Smithson-Lowe's and Daniel turned around to face him. The art dealer was already running to fat and a fondness for the better things in life was crimsoning the flesh of his face. His immaculate tailoring could not quite disguise his bulk.

'I'm sorry to have arrived uninvited like this . . . ' Daniel began haltingly, but was halted with even greater rapidity by his host.

'Dear boy, eat. Drink. That for the moment at least is all I am for. You have heard Nathan Corinth pronounce upon it. I have no other purpose. And I simply *love* to meet Orage's protegés. Are you by the way hard or soft?'

Daniel, who was already helping himself to paté de foie gras, turned back stiffly towards his host.

'Hard or soft what?'

'I was referring to your socialism. Orage you see, though something of a Nietzschean, is really rather soft on revolution. He won't, I feel, be stringing me up from the nearest lamp post. I know this somehow in my bones. But prior to consuming the fruit of my table, you might perhaps inform me if . . . '

'Hard' Daniel said flatly, wondering if the food would now be removed.

'Splendid' his host replied, and left him.

They milled. They circulated. They ate canapés with one hand while drinking first white and then red wines with the other. They gossiped. They argued. Empty silver trays were taken away and full silver trays were brought back. Glasses were filled. The volume of discourse rose imperceptibly. Imperceptibly that is for those in the midst of it. For one person standing opposite on the road outside, it was uncomfortably obvious what was going on. They were all getting drunk. And taking an unconscionably long time about it. Claire Merrill was beginning to feel distinctly chilly, beautiful though the evening might be. Her muslin dress was thin, and her cotton bodice likewise. And she had not eaten since breakfast.

She had noticed at the end of the street a public house. Its laughter spilled periodically out into the road. There appeared to be a small window on this side of it which would give a perfect view of Number Eight which she, as *poursuivante*, must keep a watch over. Could she sit in there alone? The question was no sooner asked than she was making her way towards it.

Inside the bar she bought herself a gin and water, having heard somewhere this was what people bought in bars, and sat down at a small wooden table by the window. The landlord looked over at her and shook his head. Her clean pretty features and bright clothes, together with an accent they didn't often hear in there, had classified her immediately. He leaned over the bar and whispered to one of his regulars, 'Just gone on the game. Can't have been at it a week.' The doorman from the nearby hotel turned and looked at her with great interest. He pushed his hand into his pocket to see how much money he had left.

Claire had started to discover the exhilarating effects of liquor when the diminutive drinker from the bar approached her table and smiled his clumsy smile. She ignored him but he sat down anyway and asked, 'What are you plotting then, over here in the corner?'

The curious presumption of men, Claire thought to herself, assuming all women's souls to be a transparency for them to gaze through. She leaned forward and said quietly:

'The destruction of the English royal family, actually. Using explosives. Blades. Poison. Bullets. They must all go, you know. Except for the little ones. We will put them to work on the land so they may be of some use to our species when they are fully grown. So there. That's what I'm plotting, since you were courteous enough to ask.'

He tried to look threatening.

'What, out of interest, do you think His Royal Highness King George is doing at this very moment? Any idea?'

Claire glanced at the clock on the wall.

'Making sexual advances to Her Majesty, Queen Mary' she said. 'Depending on the success of which we may or may not expect another royal celebration in the new year.'

'I'll tell you what His Majesty's doing' the little man said, well out of his depth and aware of it, 'he's working. That's what. Working.'

'Thank you so much for that uplifting piece of information. I will treasure it always.'

'Working' he said definitively, 'while some others have nothing in mind but robbing an honest working man of his wages. Uppity tart.'

With that he returned to the bar and Claire returned to her vigil.

(In point of fact King George was at that moment staring a little morosely into a large wine glass. A man afflicted with greater vanity might have found the bulbous reflection of himself that it presented displeasing. But the King retained his displeasure solely for matters of state.)

In the house of Arthur Smithson-Lowe, upon which Claire Merrill's monitoring eye was once again set, displeasure and gravity both were to be had in roughly equal proportions. Daniel Miskin, unused to drinking wine, had drunk a considerable amount – much of it poured into his glass by Arthur Smithson-Lowe personally, who was studying his uninvited guest as an anthropologist might an African tribesman. Daniel was leaning against the wall while Nathan Corinth stepped back and forth before him, lecturing. Periodically Daniel's glass would jerk red wine onto the Persian carpet. The servants had started to make towards him, but Smithson-Lowe had gestured them back.

Corinth was presently descanting on the theme of his epic work, *Medea*, some of which had been published in *The New Age* and various slim volumes. It was part prose and part verse, 'fugitive of classification' as Orage had described it, and a long way from conclusion.

'Medea remember is sorcery and distance. She is the exotic faraway who has been brought dangerously close to home. She comes from the land of slaves and bewitchment. Jason employed her gifts for safety and gold, and her body for his pleasure. She was a barbarian princess so her limbs and her psyche had not been tamed by the city. Her breasts still had eyes. And her mons was both mountain and volcano. The flame was still inside there. The molten force ready to consume.

'She is the inner sanctum of energy, don't you see? She is the gift. The inexplicable. The uncanny.

'But what does Jason do? He keeps his schemes intact, and thinks that she can be incorporated into them. That he can return to the city, to marry the daughter of urbanity. As though her power could somehow be placed into . . . negotiation. And she kills his children, as she'll kill ours, believe me, if we continue to treat her with contempt.'

'But who is she?' Daniel said, launching another surge of wine onto the carpet. 'Who is the bloody woman? I keep trying to talk to you about the oppression of real people and all you can talk about is . . . myths.'

'Your revolution is part of the myth, believe me' Corinth said. 'Its children will be murdered. The amount of terror on this earth remains constant. Only its distribution changes.'

Arthur Smithson-Lowe was distracted from this engagement by his attractively proper assistant, Marianne Morris. She was holding the photographs of the Gaudiers which she had been quietly studying in a corner.

'Arthur, these are marvellous. We must surely buy some?'

The art-dealer looked at the young lady and sighed. The time for his announcement had come earlier than expected. Like Christ at the marriage feast in Cana, he was being prompted into a demonstration of his power when he had come merely to view a celebration.

Two weeks before something had happened to the art-dealer which was set to change forever the way he looked at art, the buying of it or the selling of it. When he had inherited the gallery in Cork Street from his distant and difficult father, he had dealt swiftly with the Victorian academicists who dwelt therein, with their enormous expanses of dull colour. So much flesh halted in pseudo-classical nudity. The canvasses went quickly enough and at sufficiently remunerative prices to provide a cash-float and a little light freedom. He bought the moderns. With Miss Morris to assist him, he invested in

Parisians. The two of them went to Montmartre and saw them – Picassos, Matisses, Braques, Rovidas. Rovida was the least purchased and therefore the most purchasable. They bought a lot of *him* – most of him, in fact, since his output was limited, and was about to be definitively limited by his death.

Miss Morris thought he was wonderful, but they met him on a good night. He had washed and shaved and was determined to be good. By the time they left that evening he had enough money in his pocket to know he could afford to be very bad indeed, and had every intention of being so.

As they walked back through the streets of Paris Smithson-Lowe had felt indefinably free at last. As though he had dispensed with his father's shade. For Rovida's pictures and sculptures, with their dramatic Egyptian profiles and animalistic embraces, were instinct with an energy the art-dealer admired, though he could not put a name to it.

He had said goodnight to her outside her room and noticed the gold hairpin of a crocodile.

'They carry their young in their mouths, you know' she had said, a little tipsy from the wine he'd kept brimming in her glass. 'Clumsy in love.'

And then she had kissed him with great delicacy on the cheek.

Back in London, they had refurbished the studio in modern Viennese fashion, and then installed the Rovidas. They created something of a stir, there was no doubt of that. They were even briefly noticed by *The Times* – though with a caution verging on distaste. And there were parties and champagne and lots of bright, even brilliant people. But hardly any sales.

Then two weeks back the call had come from Duveen. Marianne had taken it and was incoherent with excitement when she told Arthur about it later. The great Joseph Duveen wished to visit the gallery and look at the Rovidas. He was finally going to step out of the Renaissance and buy modern. And they were going to supply him. They had dug their way blindfold through to a gold seam.

But Smithson-Lowe was sceptical. It did not make sense to him. Joe Duveen had cornered the market in his own field, employing the expertise of Berenson to back up his pitches with ascriptions and provenances. Why should he swerve so violently from his orbit?

When the day came, Duveen arrived with an American client whom he introduced by saying, 'This is Mr Hake of Illinois. He owns the Janus lock company. Makes millions of locks and keys every year, don't you Jim? When he has a spare week he slips over to Europe to buy some of our culture. Then takes it back with him.'

The dealer was carrying under his arm a small wrapped canvas and he asked for a tripod on which he placed the covered picture. Then he bade them explain, if they would be so kind, the virtues of the art of Lucio Rovida to Mister Hake.

Marianne Morris stepped forward and did just that. Rovida had become a passion with her now and her eloquence on the subject of his power and depth, of his visual fractures and modernity, were winning even for those of a sceptical disposition. Mister Hake, it soon became apparent, was not of a sceptical disposition, nor was he without prior information or enthusiasm of his own. Smithson-Lowe looked at the prices which he had reduced only the week before and began to wonder if he should have left them as they were.

When the exposition was complete, Duveen walked across the room and thanked his female commentator courteously and copiously for her efforts. Then he took Mister Hake by the arm and led him over to the tripod. He sat him down on the chair he had positioned before it and removed the covering from the painting he had brought. Revealed was a minor painting from a minor Renaissance artist, known conjecturally as Carlatti. It pictured Actaeon being torn by his hounds, while Artemis gloated at the side of a nearby pool.

'Mister Hake, you have heard my friends here extolling the genius of Rovida. And they may be right – they may well be right. In four hundred years we shall know. We shall know then if his savagery was justified, or an act of petulance. We shall know if his abandonment of a thousand years of tradition was bravery or mere vandalism. And we shall know if his cannibalising of other cultures was a search for sustenance or simply an exercise in plunder. Presumably we shall also know then whether such brutal portrayals of the human form engaged in certain functions was great art at the frontier, or prurience in the process of exploding. Four centuries should be long enough to show us whether or not this is a sound investment.

'Four centuries have passed already and the Carlatti has received its patina of acclaim. For the precision of its artistry, the delicacy of its touch, the dignity of its theme, and the miniature grandeur of its composition. I have here a little description by the scholar Berenson, which you would perhaps like to glance through.'

Duveen left Mister Hake to his reading and walked across the room towards Smithson-Lowe with an enormous grin on his face.

'Got him, I reckon' he said, slapping his fellow dealer on the back. 'If you're ever in Manhattan near my gallery and need a favour yourself . . . '

Mister Hake bought his Carlatti and had nothing left over for a Rovida. And Arthur Smithson-Lowe's fury gradually transmuted into something altogether different. Until here he was this evening being presented with the work of Henri Gaudier for purchase. He walked into the middle of the room and started to tap a knife against a glass decanter. Louder and louder until, section by section, the conversation closed down.

'Ladies and gentlemen. First let me thank you all for coming here tonight. The guests, expected and unexpected, have all been a delight. I would never be able to explain to you what pleasure you bring me, so I shan't even try.

'I have an announcement to make, which I had planned to postpone a little, but if life always went according to plan, there would be no poetry would there, Nathan?

'Nathan, you have asked me what point there is to my existence if I won't buy Gaudiers. It is a reasonable question, so I will answer it.

'Were I to continue as an art-dealer, then I would most certainly buy Gaudier, though whether I could sell him again is a moot point. And upon that point I have, like a captain of old, fallen.

'Sometimes it is only after taking a large step that you realise you are pointing in the wrong direction altogether.

'There is, as most of you know, a gallery on Cork Street refurbished at considerable expense – mine – and filled with modern works of art. As of noon today, however, it is not owned by your host . . . but by Nigel Hawthornden. I have sold the gallery and bought the *Kensington News*. I am now, though for the moment in an admittedly modest fashion, a newspaper proprietor.'

'Arthur' Marianne Morris was repeating with some urgency, pulling at his arm, 'I don't understand.'

'Come with me into the study, Marianne.'

He held her by the shoulders. He stared into her eyes. There were tears there which somehow perfected her. He knew she could never again be as beautiful as this for anyone.

'I had meant to tell you tomorrow. Forgive me the discourtesy. I have made it a condition of Nigel's purchase that he retain you as the director. On the other hand . . . '

Smithson-Lowe walked over to his desk and took from it a white envelope. He handed it to his assistant.

'What's this, Arthur?'

'Open it.'

Marianne Morris tore open the paper to find a cheque made out to herself from the account at Coutts of A.Smithson-Lowe for £200.

'But I couldn't take this – how could I take all this money?'

'What is it you want to do, Marianne? Forget for the moment personal matters. What is it you most want to do in the world?'

'You know that, Arthur.'

'I wish to hear you say it.'

Marianne Morris breathed in slowly and said very deliberately,

'I would like, if the talent were there, to be a painter. I would like to do this more than anything else in the world.'

'What you have taken out of that envelope is your means of finding out. If you do not choose to return to the gallery, then go to Paris. Get the studio you told me you had dreamed of. And paint. Life, you know, is so much simpler than people think. One must simply make decisions and act upon them.'

'And what about . . . us?'

'Marianne, I have no plans for marriage now. I am an ambitious man and I am about to learn a new business. There is time enough surely for us both to become successful in our different fields and then . . . schedule a further rendezvous.'

Marianne was gazing at the cheque, and those two zeroes penned in Arthur Smithson-Lowe's tiny and immaculate hand. She felt his fingers on the back of her neck, as he lifted the crocodile gently.

'Clumsy in love' she said almost to herself.

'And predatory' came the reply.

People were being helped on with their coats by the time Smithson-Lowe re-appeared. He shook hands, stroked shoulders, threatened engagements and laughed. Then he turned to stare at Daniel Miskin straddling one of his chairs, in an acute state of incapacity. Orage hovered over him, distressed, and Aubrey Innis, who had helped himself to some of his host's brandy, looked on with a curiosity which was not unkind.

'I've obviously got this wrong, Orage' Smithson-Lowe said, gesturing to Aubrey to give him a brandy too, 'but did there not used to be some connection between socialism in the north of England and temperance?'

'Used to be, yes' Orage said smiling.

'Past tense.'

'The temperance movement has moved on to the billiard halls.'

'Ah. Where does your young friend live?'

'Southfields' said Orage.

'I thought he said he lived in London.'

'Southfields is in London. It's on the underground line to Wimbledon.'

'And people actually live there?'

'Astonishing isn't it, Arthur?'

'Well, he doesn't look to be in much of a state to travel to an exotic location like Southfields on the underground tonight does he? And although the fellow intrigues me – clinically you understand, I'm a newspaper proprietor now – I can't quite face putting him up here. I have a peculiar detestation for the smell of vomit. I'll have one of my men get him a cab.'

'You'd best pay for it too, Arthur, because he won't be able to.'

'You know, despite Nathan's assertions to the contrary, I'm beginning to think I do have *some* purpose in life.'

So Daniel Miskin was despatched to Southfields and his landlady's fury. Orage made his way home, feeling a little guilty at having fed him to the lions but resolving to help him write and publish his first article. And Arthur Smithson-Lowe poured himself and Aubrey Innis another brandy from a handsome French decanter.

'I'm going to make you famous, Aubrey.'

'How so?'

'Newsprint, my lad. The only medium worth taking seriously.'

'But I'm writing my book, Arthur.'

'Well, your book can come out in my newspaper, and many eyes can see it before it ever enters a bookshop. Don't let me stop you producing any of those finely-bound editions. It's just . . . Duveen helped save me a great deal of time, you know.

I've come to understand what he's doing. There's only one thing you can sell, Aubrey, apart from the essentials in life, and that's credibility. And the major purveyor of credibility in our times is the newspaper. People buy it without even thinking about it. On the way to work, on the way home. If you wish to connect yourself by a filament of truth to the world you inhabit then you have to get your head inside one of those papers. Well, it doesn't have to be *Tit-Bits* or *The Times*, does it? Why not read Aubrey Innis about those who command? Well, why not? Your books can still come out at the end of it, Aubrey, if that's important to you. You don't have to, in any way, demean your prose.'

Aubrey Innis felt warm inside. Whether this was the result of the future just laid before him, or the excellent brandy, he felt warm in any case.

Smithson-Lowe walked over to the red patch on his carpet above which the wineglass of Daniel Miskin had oscillated. He peered down at it.

'What's that Arthur? Blood?'

'Nothing so cheap Aubrey I'm afraid. It's Chateau de Murillon '97. And that's what happens when you start sharing out your patrimony with the lower orders.

'Come back Sunday at noon. We'll have a drink and a talk.'

With his arm around his waist, Arthur Smithson-Lowe escorted his mildly sozzled friend to the door and launched him into the clear and breezy peace of London.

Should a man choose to linger against a wall on a pleasant summer night, there are a multitude of interpretations which might be placed upon his actions. If it is a woman doing the lingering and leaning, the interpretations are frequently compressed into one.

'Hello.' The voice was both cultured and hard. And it came from the dark passageway at the bottom of Smithson-Lowe's road. Aubrey stopped.

'Hello' she said again, and stepped forward. He recognised the young lady who had followed him earlier that day. She slipped her arm into his and propelled him on.

'Who are you?'

'The Queen of the Night. Do you live far away?'

'Five minutes up the road' he said and they walked on together.

Aubrey felt happier than he ever had so far in his life. He had forgotten the mild indignity of always meeting secretaries and assistants when he set out to interview commanders. He was full of drink. He was full of confidence in his own talent. He was full of the future and Arthur's paper. And now he was full of desire too. He did not ask, who, why or how? He accepted. And he took this angular, oddly beautiful young lady to his father's house in Harrington Gardens. The house, thank God, was empty of both family and servants for the weekend.

She did what she had not done before, unsure of herself initially, but discovering quickly how much power she had to bend him into her. He clawed and grappled and, even with the gin inside her, she understood this was a real force she had unleashed. So for the first time she started to understand something about power, both hers and theirs. But she did not enjoy it. She was observing and learning too quickly to abandon herself to her pleasure. Then she saw him rising into his own satisfaction, leaning on one elbow atop the world that was his by rights.

'I suppose I should give you some money' he said, smiling. An attractive smile, she thought, a truly winning smile.

'You can wait till morning' she said. 'After all, you might want to do it again and then I can charge double.'

And why not? thought Aubrey. And he lay his hand over her bony shoulder so that his fingers traced the contour of her small breast. It was different from the one he'd known before, the married one he had travelled down from Oxford to see at weekends. She had bulged where Claire contracted. His notion

25

of the female had been saturated by that affair he was now so glad to be done with. But this was different. She was agile, almost boyish. He felt like the one being taken. Of course he was paying. He didn't mind. In fact he liked it. He smiled, then fell asleep.

He woke as his wrist was tugged up by the cold steel round it and he heard the click of the metal. He tried to turn but found his other wrist had already been attached to the cold bracelet. The sun was coming through the window and Claire walked round now into the space between the window and the bottom of the bed. She was wearing a cotton bodice that ended just above her waist, and nothing else. Aubrey, hungover and confused, gradually registered that he was handcuffed to the bed.

Claire slowly pulled the sheets from the top of him until he lay there naked, his hands pulled back behind his head.

'Quite an Adonis' she said, cocking her head to one side and scrutinising him with mock professionalism.

'The pose is rather exquisite. St Sebastian perhaps but horizontal. Though that's wrong too. It's really Danae locked into her tower waiting for the man with the gold to come and have her. Or perhaps Leda pinioned, with that great swan on top of her. Or any number of nameless doxies in wars or hotels or under railway bridges. Supine there ready to be taken.'

She looked around the room. On a shelf over by the window stood a small bronze of Perseus Arming by Alfred Gilbert. She walked over and examined it closely. The figure was helmeted with one winged boot, sword curved in his hand, but otherwise naked. She lifted it up and turned it around, running her fingers along the sword, the buttocks, the minute but detailed genitalia. The anatomy was remarkably similar to Aubrey's, a fact he had himself noted as he moved it into his bedroom from the hall downstairs.

She bore the bronze back towards him, caressing it meditatively. His eyes were fixed on the delicate shadow of a triangle where her thighs met. She walked ceremoniously round the bed like a priestess conducting a grave ceremony. As she spoke she used the sculpture to trace lines across his flesh.

'Everything is yours for the taking, isn't it? And yet here you are naked and vulnerable, chained up like one of the chattels the world endlessly presents you . . . '

The bronze described an arc from Aubrey's armpit, down his side and across his belly, narrowly missing his sex. He began to stir.

'I had assumed you might actually wield some power. But I've been reading your papers through there and I realise now that you only scribble about other people who wield power. You're a considerable disappointment to me Mr Innis. And yet the world is still yours, not mine. I'm going to teach you a little lesson here about . . . those who command. It may add some piquancy to your style.

'You must have read Nietzsche – a sophisticated intellectual fellow like yourself. He asks himself a question you may remember in *The Anti-Christ*: he says, what is bad? And answers, all that proceeds from weakness. And then he asks another question: What is happiness? Do you know what his answer is?'

The sword of Perseus took a line as straight as a Roman road from the instep of Aubrey's foot to his knee and along the inside of his thigh until it hesitated finally against the soft pouch.

'His answer' Claire continued dreamily 'is that happiness is the feeling that power increases, that a resistance is overcome. How strange it is that you are hardest in vulnerability, most vulnerable in hardness.'

She edged onto the bed and so placed herself across him that he could do nothing but swerve upwards in his constriction. And this time she enjoyed her work, concentrating on the movement within herself and hearing as if from far away the curious helpless animal noises that he made.

She was gone and he slept. When he woke he felt briefly luxurious. Then the nature of his position began to impress itself upon him. He used all his strength to try to move himself and the bed. But the handcuffs were strong and the bed was heavy. And Aubrey was naked upon it and fastened – more like Prometheus now than Danae, beaks pecking away at his innards. And him with no way to relieve the urges they prompted.

❖   ❖   ❖

Alfred Merrill sat in the drawing room of his house in Stratford Road and attempted to disguise his weariness as his wife gesticulated wildly and paced up and down before him.

She was dressed entirely in black, in mourning she said for the death of their daughter's morality. This affectation irritated him almost as much as the keening pitch of her voice. Whenever this woman was in a room her husband wished to be out of it. Or wished *her* out of it. Wished her anywhere else. Anywhere.

'She is out of control. She is completely out of control. She has ceased to behave according to the standards that either you or I find acceptable. She did not come home at all last night. She is twenty years old and walks the streets like a harlot. You are the head of this household, Alfred. What do you intend to do?'

Alfred Merrill stared at his wife and tried to recognise, beneath the angular gestures and the sharpened voice, the woman for whom he had once felt such desire. In the cheek bones of her dry lined face he could still see that beautiful profile which had stopped him twenty five years before, walking over Magdalen Bridge. But desire, he knew, came only to taunt and then desert its victims. It was his job to know this. That was what he did each day in the law courts. Perceiving and administering the consequences of this very fact.

He cut his wife short.

'When she comes in, I would be obliged if you would show her in here. I intend to talk to my daughter, Lavinia. And after

I've finished talking to her, you may find your embarrassment resolved.'

She left the room muttering to herself, and Alfred Merrill KC continued with his reading of that day's *Times*.

It was half an hour later that Claire came through the door. Her white muslin dress was a little grimy and her braids half-ruined. She was whistling.

'Ladies don't whistle' her mother said, standing still at the bottom of the stairs, appraising her.

'Just as well I'm not a lady then.'

'Have you been . . . *fornicating*?' her mother asked, pronouncing the forbidden term with italicized disdain.

'I seem to remember that was one of the words you said young ladies did not need in their vocabulary, so I wouldn't know would I mother? Whether I've been doing it or not, I mean.'

'Your father wishes to see you in the drawing room. Might I suggest that you bathe and change first?'

'Are the semen stains actually visible then?'

'Oh, you are an impossible creature!'

Claire pushed open the door of the room. She held her straw hat in her hand and pulled out the remaining pin from her hair, which fell down, luxuriant and black, over her face.

For the second in which she leaned forward, then threw her head back clasping handfuls of hair to push over her shoulder, Alfred Merrill felt as though a piece of broken glass had scarred his heart. There came to him unbidden the image of his rooms in Oxford, and of a young woman standing naked before him.

'Dear Mama tells me that you have serious things to say. I am here, father, your dutiful daughter, to receive instruction.'

'Your mother would like to know where you were last night . . . '

There came a momentary silence between them in which they looked at each other frankly, even affectionately.

' . . . I however would not. There are many things about you which I have no wish to know. This, I suspect, irritates you. But

I regard your life, whether glamorous or sordid, as your own affair.

'Unfortunately, it is difficult if not impossible while living with one's parents, to live life entirely as though it were one's affair, would you not agree?'

'I would have to, I suppose.'

'Would you prefer it then if it *were* your own affair?'

'Yes.'

'Are you quite sure?'

Claire wavered here, for she had faced this implacable logic of his before, and usually lost.

'Yes.'

'Then as of one week today precisely your life shall be your own.'

'How?'

'I have bought a pleasant enough cottage on Primrose Hill. It is yours. I wish you to go and live there. I have made an allowance for you – small but sufficient. Then I shan't have to cope with your mother getting the vapours, as you put it. There are, believe it or not, matters in life of some importance other than the ladies, though the ladies like to make out always that the case is otherwise.'

'I can do what I like then as long as I don't do it under your nose?'

'I think your mother's nose is the critical area, if I recall correctly. We are trying to get you out of the hinterland of that nose, rather than this one.'

'Is that what your law means?'

'One day you will come to understand what my law means. One day when you discover what life is like without it.'

She turned to leave.

'One last question, Claire. Over my desk there usually hangs a pair of handcuffs presented to me as I think you know by Inspector Ferguson after my prosecution of the Merton Murders case. You wouldn't happen to know where they are by any chance?'

'Yes, father. They are holding the wrists of a young Adonis to a brass beadstead in Harrington Gardens. And very fetching he looks if I may say so.'

'Thank you, Claire.'

Back in her room she took off her dress and her bodice and thought briefly of Aubrey Innis as she looked at her breasts in the mirror, noticing the small blue bruise on the left one. She wondered how long he might be indisposed. Then she marvelled yet again at her father's ability to outpace her in eloquence and surprise. So, she thought, I am to be despatched with a little house and an allowance. Hail freedom then! Better start packing.

Arthur Smithson-Lowe poured the second large sherry into a glass and sipped. Where is the bugger? he thought. Finally, cross and impatient, he slammed his front door and set off at a pace to Harrington Gardens. He knew the house well. He had been entertained there many times by Aubrey's father. When he arrived at the door he was surprised to see it swinging open. He entered and walked through the downstairs rooms. A number of glasses stood on tables unwashed, but there was nothing to suggest a burglary.

As he made his way upstairs the smell became more apparent. He tried two bedrooms first. As he entered the third, the stench assaulted his nostrils. There lay the figure of his young friend Aubrey, smeared with his own faeces and turning his head away, held into place on the bed by, of all things, a pair of handcuffs.

He washed and covered him first, having pulled the soiled sheets away and taken them out the back and stuffed them in a dustbin. Then he brought one of his men with some tools to cut him free. He gave the man £10 and told him to never speak to another human being about this as long as he lived. Aubrey bathed and dressed and Smithson-Lowe took him to his club for dinner. The younger man was still shaking when they arrived but by the time they came back to Number Eight Cromwell Place, he was solid again, fortified by a good meal and the confidence of his friend, who had heard the whole improbable story, and made one joke after another about it until absurdity replaced disgust and fear in the younger man's mind.

They finished off what was left of the brandy between them and then Arthur Smithson-Lowe put his arm around the shoulder of his young friend Aubrey Innis.

'Women then, Aubrey.'

'Bloody women.'

'Best stay the night.'

In the morning, quiet in his hangover, Aubrey said:

'If there is a war, as they say, Arthur, all of this might seem so irrelevant. Your papers, my books. It might mean nothing.'

'There won't be a war, my dear. They all have far too much to lose. Mark my words, Aubrey, as a man who will be a force to be reckoned with in the newspapers of this country, there will be *no* war.'

❖   ❖   ❖

There was one of course. That very weekend the heir to the Austro-Hungarian throne was shot down together with his wife in Sarajevo. That started a creaking which grew louder and louder until in August the whole of Europe splintered apart.

The winds in the autumn drove the dead leaves back and forth in brittle frenzies over London. Some, shed from the trees of Hyde Park, rattled unconvincingly against the windows of Buckingham Palace. The fields of Flanders and France were about to receive a growing detritus of corpses. The war of attrition began piling up its mountain of statistics.

King George did not like it. It offended his notion of human dignity, and his high ideals of battle. Lord Kitchener agreed completely. When he saw the muddy mortuary that Europe was becoming he declared roundly, 'But this isn't *war*'. But still his unresistible features stared out from posters all over Britain. *Your country needs YOU.* And the eyes of the man who had avenged Gordon of Khartoum followed you about until, damn it, you couldn't very well stay at home could you?

Some did. Claire Merrill found her house on Primrose Hill much to her liking. She filled it with cats and books. As the war progressed, her wish to be involved in the world at all lessened by the day. It was a world constructed from male pride and held together with male violence. If they had to slaughter each other now to establish whose violence should be predominant, why should she do anything but close her eyes to it? She found herself following esoteric paths, she sought the occult sources of her own energy and intuition. In curious books by gnostics and theosophists she found the confirmation she required that women were closer to the centre of cosmic harmony than men. She read how men, with their protective masks of personality covering a void, set up such an impenetrable border of defensiveness that all their power was put into their hands to compensate them for the life they missed. Now the female spirit must wait patiently, as an astrologer awaits the right disposition of planets, before making a move. In this fashion, the war passed her by.

It did not keep such a protective distance from Henri Gaudier-Brzeska, whom it killed in 1915. Shortly before he died, he wrote home from the trenches that all the destruction working around him had altered nothing. His views on sculpture were exactly the same. The second and final issue of the magazine BLAST in 1915 carried Gaudier's death notice. A British newspaper, pushed now beyond the limits of its patience, commented that the joke had been taken too far when obituary notices were being written for these invented madmen.

Arthur Smithson-Lowe had still not bought any of Gaudier's work, so far as anyone knew. He reported the war in his paper, in the manner specified by the authorities, and thereby learned his trade. When the war ended, and paper restrictions ended along with it, then he would start to make his own killing.

Aubrey Innis promptly joined up, to the profound irritation of Arthur Smithson-Lowe, who thought he might be more useful on the outside of a pine box. But the older man needn't have worried. They trained Aubrey, then promptly gave him a desk job in charge of ordnance supply – they needed someone with some intelligence to do it, for it was rapidly turning into a scandal, the waste and inefficiency there. Noises had been made regarding the subject from the very top. He did not think it could last long but in fact he did his job so well, it was the only job he ever got to do. From various camps in England and France he supplied others with the wherewithal to shoot, blow up or bayonet the other side. But by the time of the Armistice he had never himself stood and faced the enemy. He felt an irretrievable sense of loss

Daniel Miskin would have been happy to tell him what he had missed. A sense of the bankruptcy of capitalist society in its savage terminal phase. Daniel was coarsened by the monotonous absurdity of battle. Obscenities, which he had previously eschewed, he now used every third or fourth word. He had joined the Royal Engineers out of curiosity for the slaughtering machines, for he knew the technology itself was innocent and would provide the basis for a new society. In the trenches he withdrew into a sullen and unloveable pride. A few of his comrades admired his stoicism, but few sought his friendship. During the whole of the war the only thing that cheered him was the news of the Bolshevik Revolution. Even then he had to read between the lines of the vitriolic official propaganda to work out what was really going on. He was wounded once by shrapnel in the groin.

Nathan Corinth would have agreed with Daniel about much of it. Certainly the bankruptcy of the civilization. The death of Henri Gaudier stunned him. And he came to hate England's dishonesty with a hate greater than he had imagined possible.

The mixture of sadism and sentimentality in the newspapers' coverage of the war overwhelmed him. Editors closed their doors, publishing houses told him he was too eccentric to print. He submitted a text to Smithson-Lowe which was returned within the week. I'm sorry, Nathan, came the reply, your commercial future as a writer is equivalent to the prospects of a disembowelled stud. The *Kensington News* is not for you, laddie, nor you for it.

Meanwhile Orage bided his time. The war did not surprise him. He remembered Queen Victoria's Diamond Jubilee in 1897. He had watched that great circus of vulgarity and chauvinism with the conviction that this huge imperial power would one day march out to war, all its misconceptions intact. But would come back different. In that respect, at least, he was right.

Marianne Morris tried to ignore the war completely, and concentrate on art. She went to Paris with her former employer's £200. And she found a small studio in Montmartre. For two years she worked for as many hours as she could keep her eyes open. Each time she finished a canvas she hung it on one of the walls. After two years the walls were full.

Marianne had spent the day at the Louvre. When she came back her eyes and her mind had been rinsed free of visual cant, for all day she had been looking at achieved perfections. It took only five minutes for her to face what she had been trying to avoid for the last six months. The paintings she had laboured over were no good. There was no vigour to her form. Her discontinuities were not the radical asseverations of Rovida, but mere failures of eye and nerve. Taking some money from under her blanket she set off to the café she knew he frequented, and which she had avoided going near ever since her arrival.

She was sitting there drinking a glass of wine when Rovida walked in. He looked dishevelled and ill. He made his way round the tables clutching a wad of drawings and trying to sell them to customers. Most of them ignored him. Finally he came to her table. He stood before her, looked into her eyes, and said:

'I am Rovida. A poor man but a true artist. These drawings here are five francs each. Please buy one so I can drink.'

He held in front of her the one on the top of the pile. It was a pencil drawing of a nude. The lines were masterly, exquisite. It had probably taken him under a minute. Miss Morris reached into her pocket and pulled out some bills.

'I'll take it' she said, 'and the other two you have in your hand.'

Rovida looked surprised. He sat down opposite her. 'You want to buy my drawing?' he asked.

'Yes,' she said, 'I do. I would also like to buy you a drink.'

Miss Morris explained over a number of glasses of wine that they had met before, but he took little notice. He said he wanted to paint her. That she was very beautiful. He wanted to buy a bottle of wine when they had finished talking here, and take her back to paint her. So she let him.

Rovida engaged in primitive rituals with his models. There was nothing aesthetically distanced about his posture. Painting occurred either immediately before or immediately after sex. The canvas received either a promise or a celebrated trophy. The man's surroundings could well have been cold stone. His studio seemed to huddle round him, lowering massive and primitive shadows across the cave floor. And the Italian hunted feverishly, taking jerks from the wine bottle, to get that image supine, eyes turned away in submission, the warm delightful pelt of abandonment. He loved women with a fierceness that overwhelmed them before they fled, or he left.

He courted Miss Morris with a species of propriety and considerable charm for the whole evening. Then he took her back to her studio. His own already had a woman in it. She took off her clothes before him, as requested, with great care. She had not told herself at any point of the evening what was going to happen. But she had not denied it either.

Lying on the rug with her legs parted, as requested, she grew colder and colder. The artist paused only to take another drink. Rovida's poisons were many: alcohol, hashish, cocaine, absinthe, ether. They acted as mnemonic devices, little triggers tripping the quotidian to let out the rush of all that the daily tedium forced back. He could not work without them.

She opened her eyes when she felt warm hands on her frosted thighs. Rovida was naked. He had finished his canvas. And they were both drunk. He had given her some hashish too. Well, she thought, what am I for? Suddenly confused images came into her mind of Arthur Smithson-Lowe, of Nathan Corinth, but they slipped away again. As well now as any other time. And she closed her eyes, conscious that this was a moment she had seen portrayed a hundred times in art but had never once enacted herself. And this man was an exceptional artist. His appetites inseparable from his achievement. And, who could know, perhaps if she could share his appetites . . .

There is a photograph, and it is one of the saddest, showing Rovida and his dealer Paul Pény on the Promenade des Anglais in Nice. It was taken in 1919. The dealer looks so dapper, his tie knotted with a firmness that could choke any stirrings of chaos or dissolution, his shoes shining confidently back towards the sun. His face is fixed by that grim joviality which announces a fellow who has got the measure of this world and knows the cunning needed to feed a family and drink a cognac, without any conflict between the two. His shoulders are elevated a full six inches above those of Rovida, who limps beside him, his draped overcoat concealing the painter's hands as though with a sad shrug. The collar is loose and the hat pushed back in retreat above a shadowed face. As an advertisement for a career, this brief exposure would not place a chisel or a brush in many hands.

He died five days after it was taken.

37

Consumptive meningitis, Marianne Morris was told, on enquiring as to the cause of his death. She wept a whole morning. While countless bodies piled one on top of another for four years, she had felt nothing but sadness at her own lack of artistic talent. Now the death of this brilliant and careless man devastated her. She decided she must return to England. With what was left of her money she bought tickets for herself and her son, the small dark boy with the bright Italian features, whom she had named Lucio.

CHAPTER TWO

Rumours of Revolution: 1926

The ancient Egyptians would bury their dead facing east, placing
the tombs over to the west of their settlements. So the ancestral
spirits might watch over the living. A sensible arrangement for
those who do not intend to be prevented in their progress by
death's punctuation. Miss Morris placed the three sketches by
Rovida which she owned, the ones she had bought from him for
five francs each, on the west wall of her room in Hammersmith.
Below them slept her small son. He had almost died in the great
influenza epidemic which had done away with twice as many
souls as the war itself. If she had lost him then, she knew, she
would no longer have been alive.

The bottle on the table was half-empty. And the face staring
over at her beloved little boy had been creased by its griefs. She
had nothing further to do with her family, her requirement for
truth proving incompatible with their offers of assistance. She
made an inadequate living taking in embroidery, sewing and
cleaning. The main expenses were the boy's food and clothes,
the accommodation and her drink. She ate little. She had that
morning finished embroidering an odd set of patterns on a large
sheet of muslin. The shapes were symbols of the Babylonian
cosmology – another job for the thin silent woman on Primrose
Hill. Miss Morris like her, though they had spoken little and she
had never told her of her previous existence before the calami-
ties. She listened now to the sweet lift and declension of her
child's breathing and thought once more of Arthur Smithson-
Lowe. She had never approached him since that night he had
signed the cheque that sealed her fate. But she always knew
that, if everything else were gone, she could turn to him finally.

Arthur was a good man – of that much she was certain.

Smithson-Lowe had been acquiring newspapers in the twelve years which had separated them. He had a feel for news and its dissemination. He understood how in a world of speed and uncertainty Everyman turned to the dailies as a sick man listens to the doctor's report: to find out the extent of the damage, to check there's still some hope – some point in proceeding.

For after the war came disaffection, strikes, a Labour government. From over the seas came the noise of Bolshevik encroachment – atheism, communism, the demolition of the family, the nationalisation of women. Smithson-Lowe understood the way these patterns of disintegration and alarm danced along the arteries of his countrymen. Zinoviev letters, the threat of foreign subversion, the sense of a world spinning ever more swiftly into madness. He knew what he was catering for, and he became more skilled by the day in doing the catering.

As he watched the events that led to the General Strike he felt a thrill of anticipation. He started drafting the leaders he normally left to his dutiful and nondescript editors. Many concerned the return to the gold standard which Winston Churchill effected in 1925. This realignment, he explained, meant punishment for the people, particularly the poor ones. The lower orders. The working classes. But necessary or not? Smithson-Lowe was a genius with the question mark. All his editorials ended with a question mark.

The mine owners said they would reduce wages, abolish the principle of minimum pay and enforce longer working hours. The miners, along with the railwaymen and the transport workers, went on strike. The government had already made provisions. And an Organisation for the Maintenance of Supplies had been formed to encourage volunteers from all those patriots who did not wish to see the land of their birthright sink into the North Sea.

Aubrey Innis had missed the trenches. Ypres and the Somme and Paschendaele were for him mere newspaper headlines. He had never himself sunk even one inch into Flanders mud. And as the poems and memoirs of the conflict started to appear he felt increasingly disqualified as a commentator on contemporary life. He had missed his blooding; the age's baptism had passed him by. The book he had been working on that day before the war was never finished. Now he divided himself into two – the columnist and the author of *The Broken Shore*. The latter would take him a long time to finish, he was sure, who could say how long? It celebrated all that obtained in these islands before the juggernaut of modern warfare had chewed up the best of a generation. Back it went to Malory and Arthur and the Chronicles . . . In the meantime he wrote his columns, *Present Profiles*. They became highly successful, much to his own surprise, and the delight of the newspaper proprietor, Arthur Smithson-Lowe, who syndicated them among his titles.

Anyway, Aubrey was ready to make a little history, rather than always recording other people's. So he finally joined up – with the OMS. Out he went onto the streets to help his country pull through its hour of danger.

What actually happened, north of the river anyway, was that London filled up with cars. Clapped-out old bangers with boards in their windows: Ask for a lift if you want one. Huge traffic jams formed. Between Piccadilly and Marble Arch a car could manage only a few yards every hour. Some of those making their unorthodox way to work were in complete sympathy with the miners. But nothing unduly serious seemed to be going on. There had been thousands of volunteers for the OMS, but few of the volunteers had any actual skills. Regent's Park became a great open air bus depot. For a couple of days there was hardly any public transport at all. Then, ramshackle, derisory and a source of humour for all concerned, the emergency services started rolling.

Aubrey's training was rudimentary. Two hundred yards under supervision and he was on his own. He found it exhilarating. The streets of London had been transformed from a neutral map into a prime site of history. He was part at last of the epic procession. Catastrophe had in fact produced something of a mood of carnival. Jolted out of their fixed routines, office workers discovered the possibilities of communication. Each day was fresh with unexpected meetings.

Aubrey did not wish to think too deeply about it. For the first time in his life he experienced the unproblematical coordination of a man of action. There were shouts from the pavement. As his hands and feet accommodated themselves to the stiff action of the gears and steering, his face relaxed into a smile. For a day he was probably as happy as he had ever been.

Even on the second morning when he had to pull up before a line of men and boys holding placards across the road in Hammersmith, Aubrey was still smiling. A policeman was riding on the running-board and climbed down with a measured frown to sort out the disruption. But the protesters were not going to shift without a fight. They were angry. A lorry they had tried to stop had sped through the middle of them and a number had only narrowly escaped being injured. It wasn't going to happen again.

The constable didn't like it. He walked back to the cab and spoke hesitantly to Aubrey.

'I think it could turn a bit nasty, sir. Stay here till I get back.'

Then off he went to find help. Behind him, Aubrey heard the sound of encouragement. Go on, they shouted, they'll all get out of the way. In front of the cab he heard something different, something he did not have a name for, yet which he in some curious manner recognised. It was the sound of a whimper turning into a shout as a crowd finds at last that its protest cannot be silenced. Aubrey climbed out of the cab and started walking away. A few jeers came from the bus behind him, but he kept walking through flesh that seemed solid now, through noise that had knitted together into a seamless sound covering the whole of London. It was only as he rounded the corner into Bridge Avenue that he realised he had been followed. The three men were the same ones who had stood directly in front of the cab. Two were young – no more than eighteen, the other at least twice their age. They formed an informal semi-circle around him as he leaned back against the wall. All three wore caps pulled tight over their foreheads so that to look at him they had to raise their faces a little. They were all smoking. Aubrey, who didn't smoke, felt suddenly as though he should.

He smiled. Now Aubrey had a most attractive smile, it had often been pointed out to him, but this time it had no noticeable effect on the three men before him. The oldest spoke first.

'The name's Brown' he said 'though you can call me Harold. And my two sons here are Matthew and Luke. Your name, if I might enquire?'

There was something both subservient and menacing in the man's tone which was new to Aubrey.

'I'm Aubrey Innis' he said with another smile, 'the newspaper columnist.'

The three men looked at each other and Aubrey knew that he had made a mistake. A bad mistake. The older man stepped forward until he was only inches from Aubrey's face.

'Why are you breaking our strike then, Mr Innis?'

'I'm not here to break a strike. Only to help my country. To be patriotic, as you might say.'

'I suppose you might say that. And a few years ago when I was in the trenches risking having my bollocks blown off, I was regarded as quite a patriot myself. You get to the trenches yourself did you, Mr Innis?'

'No' Aubrey began, 'not exactly, no, though I was . . . '

'Get it over with dad.'

It was the taller of the sons who had spoken. Wearily. Matter-of-factly. Like a man with a job to do.

The older man took hold of Aubrey's hair. Despite the humiliation, an instinct told Aubrey to take what was coming without resistance.

'We're quite good at driving buses and lorries, me and my sons. And my brother's a dab hand at digging coal out of the ground. So it's a bit of a pity that you fuckers won't let us just get on with it. Isn't it?'

The knee thudded into Aubrey's groin and, as his head swerved down, the knee met that too, and he felt the bones in his nose smashing.

'Go on' he heard the older voice say and the steel cap of a boot connected with his head. The pain exploded into blood.

'You as well, bloody well do it.'

'Not while he's lying down. I'll not hit him lying down.'

Aubrey was heaved to his feet and leant against the wall.

'I'm sorry about this' the second son said, 'it's just to keep them two happy.'

Then the iron knuckle of his glove connected and Aubrey's face fell in as his cheekbone shattered. As he slumped back down, he vomited. And then passed out.

❖   ❖   ❖

'It's not the point, Aubrey. Thugs and politicians make our history for us. Men in top hats decide on the wars and soldiers take off their flat caps and go out to fight them. I should not have to explain this to you really. Anyway, my dear fellow, at least you've given us some decent copy for when our precious printers decide to get back to work: "Innis – The Voice of a Nation – Almost Assassinated." '

'You can't print that.'

'Aubrey, I can print anything I bloody well like. As soon as the printers go back to bloody WORK.'

Aubrey Innis was lying on the sofa in the house in Harrington Gardens. It was his now. After his father's death the whole estate had passed over to him. He was bandaged and draped.

Smithson-Lowe stared at the Rovidas on Aubrey's walls and the Epsteins and Modiglianis on his tables and plinths. He whistled quietly.

'I can't even bear to ask what you paid for those Rovidas' he said. 'After all, I owned them once. I could have paid you in paintings, Aubrey. We could both have saved a fortune. But let's not get distracted . . .

'We're going national, my son. This whole business with the *British Gazette* has convinced me. A national newspaper is a greater form of power than an elected government. Everybody wants to write for the papers. Even Nathan Corinth. He has written, from Paris would you believe, a letter to the *Kensington News*. Listen to this:

Dear Sir,

I write from the relatively modest exile of Paris – I who had sworn never again to involve myself in the sewerlanes of English politics. I write only so that I may ask you and your countrymen to consider one simple question: What is money? A small question to be sure but one with large repercussions, particularly for a country determined to destroy itself for its failure to grasp the point's significance.

I may be known to a few of your readers as the author of Medea, Volumes One and Two. A different question might therefore be asked of me – by what right do I speak upon such a subject?

My own meditations in verse and prose have taken me from the beautiful terror of the classical, with its symmetry of desire and destruction, to the primary medium of communication in the modern age: money. In a rare expression of national intelligence, one of my compatriots, William Jennings Bryan, has said: Mankind is crucified upon a cross of gold. The miners of Great Britain could vouch for the truth of that.

Mr Churchill returns your benighted kingdom to the gold

standard at pre-war parity. *The consequence of this was simple to foresee – and was indeed foreseen by John Maynard Keynes: either the gold must start to leave the country by the first boat or wages must come down. Now a large proportion of every ton of coal is measured in wage cost, so why not make a good start to the business by cutting the miners' wages? And if they should demur, why then lock them out! And then talk grandly of the national interest.*

The miners will lose of course. Just as Medea lost to gold-famished Jason. But vengeance will be exacted. It always is. It is not merely in the physical world of Newton that every action produces an equal and opposite reaction. This law also obtains in the ethical, civil and political realms.

Gold is beautiful but has only the value we assign to it. When gold is raised above the needs of the children of history, an act of idolatry is committed.

Be warned: the God of wrath is approaching the mountain.

I am, Yours faithfully,
Nathan Corinth
Paris

'Rather splendid, Aubrey, I think you'll agree.'

'Are you going to publish it?'

'Certainly I'm going to publish it. In the centre pages in bold type. And since it's a letter, we don't even owe Nathan a fee.'

Smithson-Lowe rocked back and forth in self-delight. His shape approximated ever more to the spherical. This combined with his insistence on wearing long-outdated fashions in clothes gave him something of a Dickensian air. He looked as though he might have stepped from a London of fifty years before.

'You are become rotund and rubicund, Arthur.'

Smithson-Lowe twinkled and sipped his drink.

'I am fond of consuming things, as you well know, Aubrey. And the only exercise I get these days is shaking with rage at my staff once a day. But it gives employment to the tailors, letting out my trousers.'

Aubrey imagined the heavy flesh disagreeing with the waistband, and Arthur even more dyspeptic at the press of buttons.

The editor looked for a moment at the man on the couch whose eyes were once again closed. He'll never look the same, he thought to himself. That nose previously so exaggeratedly delicate had been flattened. And his face had somehow turned around its axis. The classical perfection of his features had been kicked into asymmetry and something inside him had closed down. But perhaps only for the moment. Who could say? The older man walked behind the sofa and laid his hand very gently on top of Aubrey's head.

'We very nearly lost you to the forces of history, my boy. And what, pray, have you learnt from the experience?'

Aubrey opened his eyes slowly and said without expression: 'That every action has an equal and opposite reaction.'

There were 400,000 special constables on the streets of Britain that week, 30,000 in London alone. It was perhaps just as well for the authorities that the carrying of firearms by private citizens had been outlawed in 1921 – to avert the possibility of any Bolshevik uprising here. So much incivility on the streets made for a lot of noise. A noise so loud it even penetrated the occult lair of Claire Merrill, until she found herself drawn outside to discover who was making it and why. Claire did not take papers and nor did she have a radio. She had come to regard social reality as no more than an unpleasant illusion conjured by men. Now she stumbled out into the daylight, dusty with her own oddness. And hungry. Hungry for she knew not what.

She wandered astonished through the streets. They had come alive, so it seemed, though she did not know to what she could ascribe the renaissance. She walked for hours, staring in silence at the mysterious goings-on and beginning to glean from slogans and banners and shouts what it was all about. She walked into the meeting simply because of the board outside saying: *The General Strike and Workers' Rights*. She sat down at the back and listened. With growing impatience she listened to the Labour Party and trade union representatives. They did not know whether to go forward or back, she could see that. They had no conception what to do with the power that had fallen into their hands. It was only after the main speakers had finished that the proceedings engaged her.

Daniel Miskin had his hand in the air for a full five minutes before he was called upon to stand and say his piece. The chairman thought he recognised him from previous meetings. And he was right. As Daniel rose he drew heavily on his cigarette and turned to look carefully around the room.

'Comrades' he began, 'one could be forgiven for sensing a certain confusion in the room here this evening. The elected spokesmen of organised labour have suddenly gone coy on us. Will they negotiate or won't they? Will they help to lead our workers onward to victory or backward to defeat? They don't seem to know themselves.

'I speak as a member of the British Communist Party.'

(There was a notable shuffling in the room at this point.)

'And it's no accident that many of us have been imprisoned during this dispute. We represent a real threat where the gentlemen on the platform do not. Now why might that be, do you suppose?

'The present government is made up of capitalists – have no illusions there. These aren't those old fellows with a gun in one had and a glass of port in the other. These are men whose money comes from manufacturing in the midlands; or selling the products of manufacture to the victims of manufacturing abroad. They accrue to themselves the surplus value taken from the sweat of the proletariat. Their suits may be clean but their money isn't.

'For the last six years we have endured what our wonderful free press refers to as "the pool of unemployed". Well the unemployed have stood at about a million now for some time – which is quite a big pool, as pools go. And in case anyone is taken in by the crocodile tears of the ruling class, let me assure you that the great and the good up there do not, repeat do *not*, want to see that number reduced. And why not? Because that is their cushion against a strong well-fed working class which might demand the reward due to it for its labours.

'The trade union and labour leaders are at this very moment planning to capitulate to the government, to the agents of the bourgeois state, to sell out their own membership rather than stand up and fight.

'We in the Communist Party uphold the Marxist-Leninist position. The bourgeoisie will exploit the proletariat for as long as the workers allow it. As long as they appoint supine and duplicitous leaders to speak and act for them, then they will continue to be betrayed. We are here and ready to perform our historic task. We have already received our mandate from the class struggle. We are not here to fudge another deal. And it is not reform we seek, but revolution.'

Daniel sat down and lit another cigarette. Throughout his speech there had been shouts of disapproval. Now the booes were far louder than the noise from the few people applauding. He was used to this. He expected it.

As he left the meeting he looked at his watch: seven-thirty. He didn't have to start walking yet. And he felt like a drink. It was dry work, speechifying to the unconverted. He turned into the first pub he came to, without even registering its name.

He had been sitting in front of his pint for perhaps thirty seconds when Claire sat down at the other side of the table. He had noticed her at the meeting and seen with surprise that she was one of the few who applauded him.

'Hello comrade' he said.

'Hello comrade.'

Claire had never used the word before, but it had a curious

warmth to it which she liked. And it was genderless, which she liked even more.

'Drink?'

'Yes, I suppose. What do they normally put in gin these days?'

'Tonic water, I should think. But it's a bourgeois drink.'

'I'll have one all the same.'

Daniel assumed she must obviously be in the party. She could not have approached him so casually nor addressed him as comrade otherwise. So he proceeded without any self-consciousness to talk politics immediately. The present crisis, its likely outcome, the longer-term revolutionary prospects in Britain, the sudden surge in membership, prospects overseas. Being together in the party absolved you from all social niceties. There was the struggle, and everything else was irrelevant.

Daniel drank four pints. Claire sank four gins. Daniel was not drunk, for he could hold his beer better than he ever could wine, but he was a little tipsy and enjoying himself for the first time since the strike began. Until he looked at his watch.

'Oh sod it – I mean, I'm sorry comrade. But I've got to walk back to Battersea where I'm staying tonight. It'll take me well over an hour.'

'Don't worry' Claire said calmly, 'we'll find you a bed for the night.'

If it was 'we' then it was the party, and if it was the party no questions were needed, for no protocol applied except a revolutionary one. Daniel had slept on various floors and sofas over the last few weeks. They had one last drink. God knew, they deserved it.

When they arrived finally at Claire's cottage, Daniel was surprised to find no-one else there.

'Where are the others?' he asked.

'There are no others.'

Daniel looked around the room. It was filled with strange things: curious embroideries, primitive sculptures, exotic rugs, odd books in various languages, and cats in every corner. There

50

was something odd, he sensed that. He picked up the book lying open on the little writing table and looked at its cover: *The Spirit of the Golden Dawn.*

'How long have you been with us, comrade?'

'What time is it?'

Daniel consulted his watch: 'Five past eleven.'

'Then about five hours.'

Daniel shared Claire's bed that night. And the next day on Primrose Hill Marianne Morris knocked and knocked for over five minutes while her child played among the flowers, but there was no reply. So she draped her curious embroidery across the door and resigned herself to being paid later in the week.

And the two figures in the little bed stayed motionless, unaware of the eerie Babylonian symbols stretched out over their threshold. Primitive gods in any case. And from a much earlier world.

❖   ❖   ❖

Claire Merrill left behind her old religion of the stars and embraced the new science of historical materialism with a rapidity that alternately exhilarated and exhausted Daniel. Meanwhile his old friend Orage had been travelling at some speed in precisely the opposite direction.

In 1914 Gurdjieff had visited London. Some thought him insane or at least self-concentrated to the point of implosion. But his devotees were in no doubt he was a genius. A redemptive figure. And Orage was in no doubt he himself needed redeeming.

Gurdjieff had travelled from country to country with his Institute for the Harmonious Development of Man. Half dancing troupe and half mystical cabal, this bizarre outfit needed a home. With Orage's help, permission was requested to settle in London. It was refused. Finally Gurdjieff acquired the Chateau du Prieuré at Fontainebleau-Avon.

On the 28th September 1922 Orage ended his fifteen years as editor of the *New Age*. He went off to Fontainebleau, and to Gurdjieff.

There were about a hundred of them there. A savage discipline was maintained. Early rising, hard physical labour, exhausting dance routines. These inefficient machines had to be reconditioned and put back into service. The weak spots were located. So Orage, who chain-smoked, had cigarettes forbidden him. He would be publicly humiliated by the great sage, then sent out into the garden to dig until he dropped. Only on the point of exhaustion and rebellion, would he be taken in to a fine meal and good wine. And when the smile had finally returned to his face, Gurdjieff made him dance, then heaped obscenities upon him.

He was allowed to work on nothing but the translation of Gurdjieff's musings into acceptable English. The Tales from Beelzebub told by the sage. Most men, said Gurdjieff, passed their lives in a fretful sleep from which only the truly great could awaken them. He himself was such a great one. And Orage was fit to be a disciple only if he submitted absolutely to his master's requirements.

So by 1926 Orage was in New York gathering more disciples, lecturing and sending the money back to Fontainebleau. He accepted the whole machinery of Gurdjieff's strange system. The 27 psychological types of human being, the impenetrable disguises, the nearness to death. Orage had always been an impressive public speaker. Now he looked better and sounded better and appeared almost at peace with himself.

Orage had chosen Gurdjieff knowing that his existence was at stake. All his life he had made his clever way around a void. He could only believe in the peripherals. He could see that this method of accounting was better than that one, that one sentence worked better than another. But if he ever approached his own centre, he drew back as from a vortex. He sensed the black widow in there. That dark predator with her lethal calculated movements. He knew that one day he would have to take the lid off this or it would destroy him.

Gurdjieff helped him take off that lid. And horror had certainly followed. Orage caught a glimpse for the first time of many of his true motives. He was a frightened man with great intelligence but no belief. He was fastidiously kind. But his generosity was so great because it had to compensate for the huge contempt he actually felt for most human beings. Gurdjieff saw this rapidly. He told Orage: You not know how to give. You only let others take. Let them take, you do no good: you lose and they get dependent. Not easy to give. Learn how to give, then you make other people free. (Gurdjieff spoke many languages, his grasp of most of them rudimentary but brutally effective).

Orage was a dutiful disciple. But Gurdjieff became more demanding, more outrageous. Perhaps deliberately. He was the magus – maybe he knew that it was time for Orage to return to other work. Time to get back to that drain of a world.

❖   ❖   ❖

It is of course the repetition that either redeems or destroys. Either lifts us liturgically with its daily strength, or beats us down to nothing – one damned thing after another. The daily reading is no longer from a book of hours or a missal or a bible. It is from a newspaper. Arthur Smithson-Lowe knew this and understood it. He registered the calculated dishonesty with which Churchill edited the *British Gazette*. King George was appalled at the vituperative unfairness of it, but felt his position precluded him from acting.

The *Daily Watchword* Smithson-Lowe called it, not without a certain amusement. The building in Fleet Street delighted him and the sound of the printing machines in its basement was now the only music he cared for.

'What do you think Aubrey?' he asked, having shown his friend around for the first time. Innis' newly-crooked face smiled.

'It's lovely Arthur. It's shiny and sleek and it talks in the dark and you'll obviously have to cut down the remaining forests of England to pulp all the paper that'll be needed. But what's it for, out of interest? I suppose now that Northcliffe's dead there's a vacancy. But you're not that mad . . . yet. What on earth are you going to do with it?'

'Why Aubrey I'm surprised at you. I intend to spread sweetness and light amongst the barbarians. Sweetness and light. God knows they need it.'

Light. Whether the medium of gods or humdrum traveller through a million schoolday prisms, something odd was certainly happening to it. Only five years before, Professor Eddington lectured at the British Association Hall on some of the implications of Einstein's work. Distance, it appeared, was not constant and nor was space finite.

Einstein had even abolished the ether since, as a notion, it did not help him. The sun's rays might still travel at 186,000 miles per second, and the sun itself might still be 93 million miles away, but stationary space had become mere nothingness, and there was no such thing as absolute rest. His hypotheses were proved by experiment. He became a world celebrity.

More than 100 laymen's books on relativity had reached the bookstalls by 1926 – only one of them was by the scientist himself. An English impresario even sent a telegram to Einstein offering him a three week booking at the London Palladium. An audacious mind was pressing at the limits of the universe.

What the man had established was that gravitation was not a force, as Newton had thought, but a curved field, a warp, caused by the mass of a moving body. And light itself, whether it be particle or wave, always chooses the path of least resistance through the bevel of space-time.

Light, Professor Eddington informed his exhilarated audience, can bend.

CHAPTER THREE

Darkness Rising: 1933

In the Fleet Street Office of Arthur Smithson-Lowe John Taggart looked about him bewildered. He had been brought here by his mother, a distant relative of the *Daily Watchword's* proprietor, to find out if the boy should take to writing or should seek for himself more suitable employment. Smithson-Lowe found the situation comical and at present showed no symptom of wishing to disguise the fact. To each of his attempts to ascertain the breadth of the young fellow's experience, came the reply, 'I never did that, sir. Mother forbade it.' And at each uttering of this matriarchal restraint, the lady beamed at Arthur, at her son, at the office in general and most noticeably, at herself.

His door tinkled and opened and Bobbie Morrell made her way across the office floor to lay the latest editions on the publisher's desk. The hemlines of skirts had ascended again that year and Miss Morrell's slender ankles and calves were displayed with all the prominence they deserved. John's eyes remained set upon them from entrance to exit. Smithson-Lowe smiled.

'I must now ask a question, the answer to which will determine your eligibility as a writer for this or any other paper.'

They fell silent then in this chapel of decision.

'What John is your attitude to the lower female limb?'

The boy looked for assistance to his mother and his mother stared hard at Arthur Smithson-Lowe.

'Let me see if I can be more precise. I'll summon after all these years the anatomical lore I garnered while making my line studies. What do you feel about the femur, tibia, fibula and patella of the weaker creature, man's helpmeet?'

John's expression now registered an even greater

befuddlement than previously and his mother's face tightened with incipient alarm.

'What John do you think about women's legs?'

John's mouth opened but no words emerged.

'I can tell by your haunted silence that you have been entertaining thoughts on the topic, though I have no doubt your mother would forbid it had she the power to do so. Well I can only commend you John for what I shall take to be the precocity of your wisdom. I have devoted much of the last three decades to a study of history and this grey *étude* has led me to the following conclusion: in a world riddled with pestilence, famine, catastrophe and war there are few sights more agreeable than that of a woman's legs. Unless it be perhaps the sight of a woman's breasts – considerably more difficult to obtain, I might add. Note how they rise from the ankles, often so delicate when you think of the structures they must sustain, how they flesh out in anticipation through the calf, then hurry chastely back in at the knee before abandoning themselves completely to thigh and buttock. Proffered for a man's hand to grip, like the fruit in Solomon's garden.'

John's face was now red, his mother's white.

'So go on staring my boy. And wherever and whenever possible seek to counter the abstractions of visual pleasure with the specific *plaisir* of the tactile. Do you understand me John?'

The boy's head moved slowly from side to side.

'Don't just look at their legs my lad. Grab 'em. Now kindly lead your aged crone of a mother out of here. *Rapidement*. All this talk of legs will soon have me tossing my body on hers and seeking penetration.

'*Départez!*'

Smithson-Lowe lit a cigar and once more smiled. Bobbie Morrell stood in the doorway and watched him.

'Saw them off did you?' she asked.

'Sentimentality about mothers is responsible for a great deal of misery in this world Bobbie, I've told you that before. She's entered his mind and his trousers without invitation and until he throws her out of both of them he'll never make a halfway decent roadsweep, let alone a journalist.

'Where are they?' he said after a pause.

'Outside awaiting the summons of their lord.'

'Do they look nervous?'

'No. Frightened.'

'Wheel 'em in.'

The editors and assistant editors filed through in funereal progression. They sat in their allotted seats. Not a single one crossed his legs. Arthur Smithson-Lowe had swivelled his high-backed chair round to the window. He sat staring over at St Paul's. All that was visible to his editorial staff was the back of his seat with smoke rising in intermittent swirls above it. But the voice was audible enough even while he faced away from them.

'From here gentlemen I can see the site of St Paul's Churchyard and St Paul's Cross. In earlier and less sophisticated times than these, preachers would preach there and poor men would gather round to listen. For hours at a time, I gather, a learned theologian could discourse on relatively abstruse topics concerning grace and salvation, free will and the predetermined fate of the individual soul. And these unlettered fellows would be spellbound. The force of oratory you see. The power of the greatest of all languages to charm and enrapture when efficaciously deployed.

'I daresay I flatter myself somewhat but I've always liked to think our newspapers at their best had taken over where St Paul's Cross left off. We are here to capture the imagination of our people through the astute use of our pens and our typewriters and the chappies with the hot bits of metal.'

Smithson-Lowe swivelled his chair round slowly till he faced them. He leaned forward and lifted a copy of last week's *Watchword* from the tray where he had placed it.

'So when I read on the front page of Wednesday's edition this immortal piece of prose, "Mrs Simmonds, whose dog had died the previous summer, cannot explain her cat's mysterious disappearance" I am hardly surprised that the *Express* and the *Mail* appear to be selling rather more copies than we are.

'Are you surprised Henderson?'

The editor reached his left hand up to the knot of his tie, then straightened his spectacles. Then coughed.

'It was I think you yourself, sir, who told us – eloquently, if I might say so – never to forget the curiously intense relationship the English have with their animals . . . But I freely admit it was hardly the strongest story of the . . . '

'Then why was it on the front page? WHY?'

The publisher was shouting now and both fists came down with a mighty thump on his table. These outbursts of proprietorial rage were originally entirely contrived. Then Smithson-Lowe had started to slip into such theatrical routines so effortlessly that contrivance was no longer needed.

'The only superlative writing I can count on every week is from Innis. The rest of these scribblers you employ with my money are pigmies. Now shape up your staff Henderson. I mean it. My patience is running out by the day.'

They raised themselves out of their chairs and straightened their jackets. They emerged into the corridor exchanging fierce whispers.

'Innis again. Who's going to have the balls to tell him who writes the Innis column these days?'

'Whoever it is will be through the front door, integrity intact, five minutes later.'

'He can do no wrong then?'

'He is the jewel in the *Watchword's* crown. Age shall not wither him nor custom stale his infinite variety.'

'He's got a nice motor too.'

Thirty minutes later Bobbie Morrell re-entered Smithson-Lowe's office. He looked at her silently while caressing the cigar in his mouth.

'Well?'

'There's a woman outside insists on seeing you. I've tried the cold shoulder. I've tried getting her to make an appointment. She won't go. Says you'll see her if I only announce her to you. Her name is Miss Marianne Morris and she is not about to win our deb of the year comp.'

Smithson-Lowe swivelled his chair back round so he was facing the window.

'Show her in.'

Marianne was led to the seat nearest the door. There was silence in the room fractured only by the traffic and the shouts outside. She saw the smoke rising above the leather back of the chair. Smithson-Lowe noted a single gull dipping through the air a hundred feet away. He swivelled round slowly.

It was clearly her, though had he seen her on the street he would have passed her by unknowing. But the ruin of her face still carried the recognisable features the years had spoilt. She was thin to the point of debility, her clothes too old and too worn. Her hands, although cupped in her lap, were noticeably trembling. Smithson-Lowe walked wordlessly over towards her. Looking down he saw that the ribbon which still pulled her hair back from her face so severely was grimed with sweat-marks. And he could smell the drink. On her breath, on her clothes. On her skin.

He walked to the cabinet and spoke softly as he opened it.

'Ah my dear, the last time I saw you the lights were about to go out all across Europe. And now I fear Marianne the light has gone out not a little in you. Permit me to rekindle it?'

Marianne looked up finally with tears in her eyes. The soft deep sound of Arthur's voice had brought back the time, two decades before, when life seemed all possibility. He had become more corpulent and somehow more polished. Brilliantined and glittery. He was holding open the little door behind which lay a miniature forest of bottles.

'Anything you care for Marianne?'

'I don't know Arthur . . . I keep meaning to . . . '

'I find a little gin around this time of day is often something of a pick-me-up. It's such a clean anonymous sort of drink.'

He was already handing her the glass. She stared down into the contents, as the froth settled to transparency. He clinked his glass against hers.

'Have a little snifter, eh? Make you feel a little better.'

Her hand shook as she lifted the glass to her lips. But the contents she downed in one gulp. He took the glass from her and refilled it immediately, this time making sure there was more liquor in the mix. Smithson-Lowe liked to establish quickly the weaknesses of those with whom he had to deal. He sat on the front of his desk as she sipped and grew calmer.

'It's good to see you again Marianne, though I sense that life has dealt you some harsh blows. What has brought you to my door?'

'I need help.'

'What is the nature of the help you require?' He had once more lifted the empty glass from her hand and was replenishing it with professional fluency.

'It's my son Arthur . . .'

'You have a son?'

'Yes. Lucio. He is sixteen.'

'But you are still Miss . . .'

Some anger flared in Marianne, not directed at the publisher but at her family, at every petty official who had ever raised his eyes to say, And you are *Miss* . . . ?

'Yes I'm still Miss and now I always will be Miss. And I was Miss when I took my clothes off for Rovida, and Miss when I had his son and now I'm Miss here asking for you to give me some money so I can get my boy out of prison. Miss. Miss. Miss.'

Smithson-Lowe was genuinely surprised, more surprised than he had been since he had realised that Aubrey Innis really had come to prefer women again – insofar as he could be described these days as preferring anything. Some soft and hidden part of him he wished to forget had been slapped unexpectedly.

'You had Rovida's child? But surely he died soon after we . . . '

'I was his last fling at life Arthur. And now his son's in Wandsworth locked up and I want him out. He's not a bad boy but he's in with a bad lot.'

Holding back the tears she said *sotto voce*:

'He could have been our son Arthur. So easily. It might have been you and me together.'

Smithson-Lowe turned swiftly away. In a second he was at his desk, pulling out papers, writing busily.

'I'm going to help you Marianne. But not with charity. Charity only debases and debauches. Why, the last time I was charitable towards you . . . well, never mind that now. You need advice, lawyers, money. And you can earn it too. If you would like to sign this little contract here, giving me the rights to publish your story in my newspaper, then we'll get to work. There!'

Smithson-Lowe held the sheet in front of her. In his other hand the pen. He was smiling.

'Promise me Arthur.'

'I promise. When did I ever let you down?'

Marianne Morris scratched her wavy and uneven signature onto the bottom of the paper. Smithson-Lowe whisked it cheerfully away and dropped it into his drawer.

'We need photographs Marianne. Of you with Rovida. Of the boy when younger. We'll take our own shot of you in your present plight and in your own . . . surroundings. And as many details as possible. I'm a busy man so you can give them to my assistant Miss Morrell.'

Smithson-Lowe picked up the phone on his desk.

'Bobbie, come in for a moment would you? This calls for a drink I'd say. Let me fill that glass of yours up until it runneth over . . . Ah, Bobbie. You've met Miss Marianne Morris of course briefly. But I should explain that Marianne and I were once very close. In fact oddly enough Marianne once performed the same indispensable services for me as you yourself do now.'

Bobbie looked at Marianne and noted the same dark hair, the same trim boyish body as herself. She thought briefly and unnervingly how Marianne must have looked twenty years before.

'You must take Marianne for a good lunch with the best wines and keep ready that notebook of yours where you scribble down all those shorthand hieroglyphics I can make neither head nor tail of . . . Then get photographs of Marianne and her little boy and also the great artist Rovida with whom she . . . liaised. Also please to find out the details of the difficulties Marianne's son appears to have found himself in.

'I'll be out for much of the day for I'll be meeting Aubrey for lunch and you know how legendary *his* lunches have become. But I'm anxious we should have this story before the public as soon as possible. This is twentieth century history after all. Art and suchlike matters. So perhaps you could bring the results of your day's work to my home this evening. And we'll continue there.'

Bobbie Morrell leaned her head slightly to one side and looked into Arthur Smithson-Lowe's eyes.

'So it will be another working evening will it sir?'

'Oh I should think so Miss Morrell, yes. Until quite late I shouldn't be surprised. After all, we both have a living to make, do we not? Man that is born of woman . . . etceterah etceterah.'

'And the new arrangements, sir, regarding my position? Have we progressed any further with them?'

Smithson-Lowe looked back with undisguised irritation.

'Shortly. When I say something will happen, it happens.'

Marianne Morris stood up a little unsteadily and kissed Arthur Smithson-Lowe gently on the cheek.

'You're a good man Arthur.'

As Bobbie turned to close the door Smithson-Lowe said curtly:

'I want Hington here now.'

'He's out on a story.'

'Then get him off the story Bobbie. I want him in here before I go.'

The photographer was found a half hour later by a breathless underling and told to report to the publisher's office. He turned up still holding his five-by-four.

'Problem?'

'No. Bobbie's doing some research. Go with her. The woman she's with will be plastered by the time lunch is over. Go back to her apartment after. I want a shot for the centre pages Hington and I want it sordid.'

'What kind of sordid?'

'Whorish sordid. Slut sordid. Soused mummy on the game sordid.'

'And for this I get taken off a flooded confectioner's at Farringdon?'

'Out.'

Arthur Smithson-Lowe lit another cigar. He swivelled ten degrees this way and ten degrees that. He stared over towards St Paul's and hummed gently to himself. Soon the shape of Aubrey Innis' Bentley would cruise down the street and stop in front of the *Watchword* building. Now for these few moments Arthur Smithson-Lowe was as close to happiness as his world permitted.

❖   ❖   ❖

'You're telling me the prim young lady with the little boy thighs who was your assistant in Cork Street went off to Paris and became Rovida's mistress? And had his child?'

'That's what I'm telling you.'

'It is at the least extraordinary Arthur.'

'It is very nearly incredible Aubrey.'

'And how does she look now?'

'Bloody awful.'

'What made her come over your trench after all this time?'

'Her son's been nicked.'

'What for?'

'Don't know yet. Bobbie's spending the day with her and will report back to me this evening.'

'A working evening then?'

'Absolutely.'

'At home?'

'One requires some comfort.'

The eyes of Aubrey Innis left the road briefly and met those of Arthur Smithson-Lowe.

'It's always surprised me Arthur that you of all people should have picked an American to be your personal assistant.'

'Well, there are advantages you know. They have a certain *brio*, a certain briskness and despatch about them I find refreshing. They make it their business to find out what it is you want and then they . . . give it to you. That appears to be their philosophy.

'Bobbie incidentally will not be my p.a. much longer. She has always had other ambitions. More in your line.'

'She wants to write?'

'Do you know anyone who doesn't? It seems to be the disease of the age.'

'And how much chance does she have of fulfilling this ambition in your kingdom?'

'A very good one as a matter of fact. A very good one indeed. Bobbie really is a most capable young lady. She even mentioned to me the other day that she knows of a surgeon in New York who could probably straighten out your face for you.'

Aubrey Innis slipped the car into third and pressed his foot hard on the throttle. The wind blew a flicker of flaming ash from Smithson-Lowe's cigar into his left eye. They had Richmond Park almost to themselves and Aubrey was enjoying his motoring.

He had bought it in 1928, the same year the Bentley Four-and-a-Half Litre had won the Le Mans. It had cost him £1,295 and he was intent on extracting value from every penny. Now the car cruised sweetly down to the forefront of The Old Bridge Restaurant. Signor Bertolli himself was waiting at the door.

'Mr Arthur. Mr Aubrey. Always such pleasure. Your usual table by the window.'

'So we can dream about journeys.'

'And contemplate the latest tide in the affairs of men.'

They were disrobed and seated. Turning on an impulse Smithson-Lowe called out to the owner:

'Did you ever know Lucio Rovida?'

'No' came the reply 'but my brother did. Bad man. Drink drugs women.'

'And painting' Aubrey said sourly.

Arthur Smithson-Lowe turned his look carefully back towards Innis.

'His otherwise sordid life redeemed by his art you mean, Aubrey?'

'I mean nothing of the sort. Drink drugs women, bad man' he said in a mock Italian loud enough for Bertolli to hear and the waiters to flinch. 'We know fellows at the Garrick who are worse than that. Rovida was just unlucky. But he had talent and left something of value amidst all this . . . dross of ephemera.'

'Perhaps. Though Joe Duveen thought otherwise and managed to talk Jim Hake into agreeing with him. And I do sometimes wonder if perhaps Messrs Hake and Duveen might not have been right after all.'

'I don't believe Duveen ever questioned Rovida's talent – merely his culture.'

Bertolli was back dispensing menus.

'Drink gentlemen? Signor Innis does very good imitation of my accent, no? You really are very much the entertainer.'

The padrone was not smiling.

'That's what Arthur here pays me for, isn't it Arthur? To entertain the masses with my finely-honed style. I'll have a whisky. Large. No soda.'

The men's eyes met over their drinks, then glanced oppositely away.

'On the subject of your finely-honed style, Aubrey, I can't help noticing a certain formulaic quality creeping in of late. The profiles seem to have grown a little tired.'

'Maybe they've reached the end of their natural life Arthur.'

'Maybe they have Aubrey. Or perhaps the fact that they're now written by young Paddy Kenlon has something to do with it. What do you think?'

A gap widened between them, an ellipsis of more than words.

'I draft the final version.'

'You add the odd adjective, delete the occasional conjunction and substitute an intermittent comma. I know my lad because I've seen the drafts. You must be the best paid quester for *le mot juste* in Europe. Flaubert would have envied you.'

'If you want me off the paper Arthur, then say so.'

'My dear fellow, the *Daily Watchword* without the Innis profile? Unthinkable. Why, we have become a national institution together.

'But you are tired Aubrey and you need to finish that book of yours surely? After all it's been . . . what, ten years and still no . . . '

'Don't tell me how long I've been writing my book and I won't tell you how long you've been fucking your assistants . . . '

Aubrey's voice had risen in a quick surge and waiters were once more dipping their heads and exchanging frowns.

'Well goodness me, Aubrey. What a temper you have these days! All I'd meant to suggest was that it's time for you to finish your book. And I'd like you to do so. On full pay of course, for you will not technically have left us at all.

'Which is to say that I'll take over the direction of the column now you've trained up Kenlon to do the dirty work. You can't create art at the same time as churning out journalism. We both know that. They're incompatible – you've said it yourself a thousand times.'

Smithson-Lowe placed his hand over Aubrey's.

'And that's why you haven't finished your book. It's the only reason, I'm sure of that. So now you can climb into that splendid motor of yours and re-trace Arthur's journey – it was something like that if I recall. And scribble scribble scribble, eh Mr Gibbon?

'Be assured, the Innis column will be safe with me . . . We might even change the format a little.'

There was another silence. Of weariness, of unavoidable reconciliation.

'All settled then Aubrey?'

'All settled then Arthur.'

A cautious smile met a jubilant grin.

'I've decided this lunch is on me. Let's have some champagne. And let's toast the success in advance of *Broken Shore* – that is what it's called isn't it?'

'Not any more. Now it's called *Merlin*.'

'Merlin? The Welsh wizard?'

'No, that was Lloyd George.'

'I thought he was the Welsh goat?'

'Well I suppose we all have trouble with a Vivienne of some description . . . '

'You know Aubrey I don't intend this cruelly, but are you sure you don't have too much of a sense of humour to write one of these truly modern works?'

Smithson-Lowe pulled from his pocket the little green book which Innis had given him at their last meeting, T.S.Eliot's *Poems 1917-1925*.

'I mean this chap for instance . . . Isn't he some sort of editor now, God help us?'

'*The Criterion*.'

'What's the circulation of that then?'

'Couple of hundred.'

'Ah, so the *Watchword* is safe for the moment.

'He does rather enjoy his obscurity doesn't he? I mean one of these poems actually starts . . . ' Smithson-Lowe hunted through the pages. ' "Polyphiloprogenitive." That's the whole of the first line, Aubrey. Doesn't have quite the same ring as "Shall I compare thee to a summer's day?" as first lines go does it?'

'It's not one of his finest . . . '

'All right, let's take *The Waste Land* then, shall we? Anthem of a doomed generation, I gather.'

'*He* wouldn't say that.'

'I daresay he wouldn't. Even so. Aubrey the whole thing's broken into bits. It's not even all in English. One minute there's a hermaphrodite looking back on a few evenings of remarkably dull sex, then some half-crazed society bint wittering on at her languid husband, then a Lebanese merchant after a dirty weekend. A drowned sailor. An Indian mystic getting damp . . . Then when I read the notes at the back (and that's ominous, you know, poems with notes – I never got through *The Dunciad* at school because of that) I realise most of the best lines in it aren't even written by him at all. He swiped them.

'I know how to put together bits of everything and call it a newspaper but I don't expect people to do that in poems. Aren't these fellows supposed to have a voice – rather than merely imitating everyone else's? The man's a ventriloquist.'

'No, I'm sorry but the older I get the more I march with Duveen and Hake.'

Smithson-Lowe smiled at Innis who knew only too well the futility of opposing him in this mood.

'Now Aubrey what is *Merlin* about? And this time make sure you don't have to explain your explanation. If I'm to finance its completion at least I'm entitled to know what species of fish flesh or fowl it is.'

'It is a meditation' Aubrey said carefully 'on how we create the past out of the ruins of the present.'

'Another real rib-tickler, eh?'

'I doubt you'll be serialising it.'

'Will Eliot in the *Criterion*?'

'I . . . I don't know. I suppose not.'

'And why Merlin? Let me think. Didn't he bring the stones over from Ireland for Stonehenge?'

'He did. He was one of our first creators of public spectacles. An impresario *avant la lettre*. Some points of contact after all, Arthur.'

'You still haven't answered the question. Why Merlin?'

Aubrey took a long pull of his drink and resigned himself to his vulnerability.

'He's the filament between two worlds. His pagan magic creates the Christian prince. He's the lifeline between the green man and the crucified god. And he stays imprisoned to this day, invisibly imprisoned, in thrall to the erotic.'

'And his magic . . . continues?'

'Possibly. In poetry, possibly.'

Smithson-Lowe snapped his fingers.

'Then he has something in common I believe with Nathan Corinth's Medea.'

Aubrey Innis looked crossly at his empty glass.

'The wine appears to have stopped flowing in this mead hall. Yes, I daresay he has something in common with Medea, and plenty of other figures besides. But my book's not like Corinth's at all.'

'Is he any good then, old Nathan? Give me your candid view.'

'He may be our finest poet. It's too early to tell.'

'But half of it's not poetry. It all keeps collapsing into prose.'

'That's why he may be our finest poet. He found the form he needed.'

'And all those obscenities. Is that necessary?'

'He claims the poet who cannot carry his necessary freight of obscenity, cannot contain the age in his work.'

'That's what old Nathan says is it? Now tell me, who narrates Merlin? Whose voice am I going to have to listen to?'

Aubrey Innis let his theme take over from his caution.

'There are three voices. The first is that of John Leland, antiquary to Henry the Eighth as he tours Britain at the time of the dissolution of the monasteries, collecting together the matter of Britain. The second is Taliesin in Logres, lamenting the dissolution of the fellowship of Camelot. And the third is the waking mind of Arthur, rising through the ages of his slumber in the cave.'

Arthur Smithson-Lowe removed the finger from his nose.

'Aubrey, it really is a bloody modern work then? Broken into bits is it?'

'At the moment.'

'My brain aches and a drowsy numbness pains my sense before I've even clapped eyes on the damn thing. I do however intend to enjoy my lunch.'

And enjoy their lunch they did. Marianne Morris enjoyed hers too, every mouthful and glassful. In fact as the meal proceeded her contentment turned into something approaching gleeful mania. Hington was bored and, unusually for him, embarrassed. Bobbie Morrell found the occasion distasteful but continued to take notes as instructed.

Three cabs drove by after they had helped Marianne out of the restaurant. The fourth was having second thoughts as they manhandled her into the back but Hington thrust a ten shilling note into the driver's hand and told him the address. She had already passed out by the time they arrived.

Bobbie helped Hington carry her inside after they had extracted the keys from her pocket. Then she walked around the rest of the flat and collected a couple of photographs from their frames, pausing only to admire the Rovida sketches that hung above the bed. When she came back it was to see Hington arranging Marianne's limbs after a painting by Ingres, her skirt having been pulled towards her thighs, and the top three buttons of her blouse unfastened.

'What exactly do you think you are doing Hington?'

He turned towards her, still on his knees on the mattress.

'I am carrying out the instructions of the man we both revere.'

'Those instructions being?'

'He wants a picture of her looking like a tart. Not' he said, on his feet now and walking over to her, 'a luscious young tart of the sort we'd all cheerfully hand our wages over for.' His hand lay gently against Bobbie's cheek, then his finger traced down towards her breast. 'Not the kind of tart only the fellah at the top of the pile gets to see outside of her knickers. But a raddled old bitch you've got to keep the light off till you've done with. Now excuse me – I have work to do. Each to his own whoredom, Jenny.'

Hington started to check his flash and Bobbie walked out of the flat. Out into the streets of Hammersmith busy with shops and lorries and exhaust fumes and troublesome children. Not as busy as New York where she was born. But busy. She walked aimlessly until she came to the riverside and stood there against the rail, leaning over the water. Ebb-tide. A barge was moored immediately downstream of her, a baby's washing hanging from its spar.

'I do hope this is worth it' she said to herself. 'I do hope these sacrifices that sometimes seem greater than life itself are worthwhile. And the first thing I'll do when I'm promoted is fire Hington.'

At seven thirty that evening she rang Arthur Smithson-Lowe's bell. He opened the door himself, draped in the black silk dressing-gown he wore after his bath. She walked past him without speaking, upstairs and into his living room. She poured herself a martini and sat in the large armchair, kicking off her shoes and raising her legs onto the cushion. Her notebook lay open on her lap.

Smithson-Lowe sat opposite her.

'So?'

'So she goes to Paris with your cash fresh in her paw. I never realised you were such a patron of the arts, Arthur. I do hope you got your money's worth before her departure, though she claims to have remained intact prior to Rovida. Anyway, she paints and paints. Lives like a nun who's taken the veil of the muses. Goes to the Louvre one day and hey-presto the kid catches on. They've all got talent. She's got none – a fact I strongly suspect had not entirely escaped you when you philanthropically made out that cheque. So instead of doing what we American gels do in the circs – namely a spot of re-training as a nurse perhaps, or a teacher, or a soda-pop jerk – she goes off and finds Rovida. Does the deed of darkness with our ramshackle but still randy maestro, then continues as one of his innumerable pieces of skirt for eighteen months. Takes to the bottle and several varieties of dope – all in imitation of her mentor, you understand. All for the cause of art. Just before he croaks our vigorous Latin manages to impregnate her.

'And so she returns to dear old blighty penniless and in need of a friend. Her family offer to take her in so long as she plays the widow and stays home knitting with mum. She tells them to screw. Gets by somehow, hand to mouth, bottle to bottle, and brings up young Lucio – Lucio Morris doesn't have quite the same ring to it does it? Anyway little boy gets to be big boy and turns into a bundle of trouble both to himself and to his faded English rose of a mother. She says he's been set up. But I doubt it. While you were out carousing with your old pal Innis I dropped into Wandsworth jail to improve my English.'

'And?'

'And I get the impression young Lucio, or Lucky as he prefers to be called, might turn into one of the more resourceful criminal minds of the next decade.'

'You saw him?'

'I saw him.'

'And?'

For the first time she paused and sipped her drink.

'He's strange. Sinister. Rather beautiful.'

'Can we get him off the charges?'

'Possibly. Probably. Spend enough money. Are you sure you want to?'

Smithson-Lowe walked over to her chair and knelt in front of it as he unfastened his gown.

'Well' he said 'a deal is a deal after all.'

She remained motionless as he pressed and kneaded, stroked and unbuckled.

'On the subject of deals Arthur, when does my payoff finally come, since you take yours with such forceful regularity?'

'Next week in the middle pages.'

'You're serious?'

'I am always serious Bobbie. You should at least know that by now. And tonight I must celebrate with my new star writer,'

She stood and let her skirt slide to the floor, then she unbuttoned what was still buttoned of her blouse. She moved back to where he knelt on the floor and pressed the top her thigh against his cheek.

'Circe or Penelope?' she said.

'Oh both I think. On such a night as this, I rather think both.'

'I am coming to the conclusion – speaking as a colonial you understand – that you Brits are a nation in terminal decline.'

❖   ❖   ❖

Daniel Miskin read once more the note that Claire had tossed before him onto the table.

> She died at sea in a state of what has been described as chronic depression. The verdict will undoubtedly be misadventure, though frankly I fear a more truthful description would be suicide. I know how busy you are but would obviously be most grateful for a visit at this time of our grief.
>
> Love, Father

'You must go to see him. Immediately.'

Claire turned slowly from the window and looked at him with that expression of irrecoverable disappointment which seemed to have intensified at the same rate that his own devotion to her had deepened.

'There is a party meeting this evening for which I have not yet finished my preparation. Of some importance I think you might agree Daniel. What was it you said last week? Now that Hitler has taken power we are in the final stages of the struggle. The final stages. No more compromises. Fascism or communism. Choose before the destruction of all choices.

'Mother is now dead, however it happened. Gone to bemoan her fate to the fishes, no doubt. Please don't expect any petty bourgeois sentimentality from me. Your problem Dan is you don't believe your own philosophy. She was a rather stupid woman if the truth be known. A handmaid, no more, to my father who now feels racked with guilt at having goaded her on all these years to her own destruction. Well I see my father once a month, as you know, and today is not the day.'

'You mean you collect a cheque from him once a month.'

'Which provides the wherewithal for us to fight a revolution. Perhaps you could recommend a better use for expropriated wealth?'

'I'm only saying your mother's dead whatever you thought of her, and your father's in grief, of some sort. You could at the least go to see him.'

'If you have such strong feelings about these middle-class proprieties, Dan, you go. I have work to do.'

Daniel decided to walk. It was a fine day though chilly. He felt mildly nauseous as always after quarrelling with Claire. Something relentless in her had taken the name of Marxism-Leninism but he was not sure what it was or where it came from. He walked for an hour before he came to the house in Harrington Gardens.

As he entered the room where Alfred Merrill sat, Daniel registered the frailty that was beginning to make its way through him, a new look of vulnerability about the eyes. Mr Merrill rose and took Daniel by the hand.

'It's good of you to come. Claire is . . . '

'Desperately trying to finish something . . . If she can . . . later . . . '

'I understand.'

Alfred Merrill stared steadily into Daniel's eyes, then he reached out a hand and touched Daniel's brown tweed lapel.

'It could have been cut for you Daniel. It fits perfectly.'

'It's good of you to let me have them. All the clothes you give. It helps greatly.'

'Well anything I can do of course towards your . . . work. You don't feel overdressed, ever?'

'I keep my jacket buttoned at party meetings so no-one gets to see the label.'

Both men smiled for a second. They looked related in some way, both in the same three-piece suit, both with the same make of tie, the same brand of shoe. Claire had suggested it on one of her visits to her father, since their height and build were so similar. Alfred Merrill acquiesced in her suggestions as always, and so took to handing over to her the clothes and shoes he no longer wore. And back on Primrose Hill Daniel Miskin put them on.

'I'm sorry' Daniel said at last. 'I'm sorry about your wife.'

'Thank you Daniel. Thank you too for the courtesy of your visit. I appreciate such things. It's a cold day for it too, so come into the next room and I will pour a drink for you.'

They sat in silence as the long-case clock thumped out the seconds. The walls of the room were lined with the leather-bound volumes detailing that practice of law from which the older man had so recently retired. Mr Merrill was looking through the window at the shifting tops of the trees as he spoke.

'Forgive the impertinence of my question, but have you and Claire ever considered marriage?'

'Claire won't' Daniel said matter-of-factly.

'Ah! Claire won't. No, I can see that. A bourgeois institution?'

'A machine for the reproduction of labour. A capitalist racket propped up by ideology.'

'And yourself. What do you think?'

'I would have married Claire at any time since the night we met.'

Alfred Merrill once more looked carefully into Daniel's face. When he had first met him, it had been hard for him even to be civil. He could see nothing but Claire's gesture in choosing this northern revolutionist with his awkward manners and curious accent. But there was something at the heart of Daniel – a strength, an unconscious propriety which transcended class – that he had come to respect from the gleanings he caught of it at their infrequent meetings.

'I have always wanted to ask you Daniel but with Claire around . . . Well, never mind. How can I put it? What are you fighting for really? To what are you and my daughter devoting your lives?'

Daniel felt defensive now. The forensic precision of the intellect of A.Merrill KC had a legendary quality for him. It was the only thing in the world he knew of which was able to intimidate Claire. Yet he liked Mr Merrill. He had liked him instinctively from the first time they ever met. Respect for the enemy, he had said to Claire. Untruthfully.

'You'd best give me another drink if you really want the answer to that.'

Mr Merrill poured the drinks. They sat for a moment in silence. Then Daniel began.

'I was brought up in the north of England as you know. Raised in a working-class family. I shan't tire you with all the details. But my father died when I was twelve. Of pulmonary emphysema. Which to us was just a posh way of saying that he was killed from swallowing pit-muck. My mother was an unhappy and embittered woman whose only hope in a dark life was that I should get out of the class I was born into and enter another. And I studied. Studied hard. Got my engineering qualifications. But the idea of just escaping myself, looking out so entirely for number one, somehow upset me. What about everyone left behind? What about the ones who couldn't escape?

'I came across Orage, socialism, Marxism finally. Gradually things started to focus. I started to make out the economic system and how the political system sits on its face like a mask to disguise it. I understood that if the working-class can seize the power at its disposal and use it in a revolutionary manner, it can end its oppression. That's what I'm fighting for. And Claire too – I think.'

'Thank you for being so frank with me. Am I right in assuming I'm part of the oppressor's class with which history must dispense?'

Daniel looked uneasy. He took a sip from his glass.

'There's no need to feather my fall, Daniel. It is after all history which either will or will not dispense with me, rather than your good self.'

'Your skills could I'm sure be of great use in any society, but not the bourgeois system of law in which you operate.'

'So the present system of law is to be abolished?'

'Yes.'

'And replaced by?'

'Revolutionary tribunals of the workers. The present system operates to consolidate the existing distribution of wealth under capitalist conditions. A different historic configuration would require a radically new form of justice administered by the newly dominant class, the proletariat. As in the Soviet Union at present.'

'You believe the system of justice that obtains in the Soviet Union to be more equitable than this one, do you?'

'Yes.'

'That's not I'm afraid the impression I've received. You heard I take it a few years ago of the so-called kulaks . . . '

'Yes, I know all about the countless lackeys and counter-revolutionaries it has been necessary to re-organise or even in some cases dispose of. And the lies and propaganda the capitalist west generates to terrorise the workers here against taking their own road to socialism. I also know that as the hunger marches increase in size so do the crowds at the Henley Regatta. I doubt your system of justice is likely to do much to alter that. And I remember seeing the miners after they'd been defeated – after six bloody pointless months out by themselves. I saw them staring at stationary pitwheels in Barnsley and scavenging coal from the rail-lines in South Wales – coal they'd pulled out of the ground with their own hands. I saw the looks in the eyes of their wives and children and I knew they'd never forget this. And neither will I.

'This system is built for war. Class war, imperialist war. There was unemployment in Sheffield before 1914, but not once the war got going. I handled the shells and the guns and the bayonets. Firth's, Hadfield's and Brown's. But they're all on short time again now. What kind of system is it when you only get full employment if everyone's trying to slaughter everyone else?

'Adolf Hitler has been put into power in Germany by the industrial powers – to save them from revolution. And I have no doubt either that if the bourgeoisie in this country is faced with the same choice it will make the same decision any day. Fascism against communism. You only have to read the leaders in *The Times* to see that.'

Daniel stopped. He had become heated. He looked at Alfred Merrill's haggard and weary face and he remembered the occasion of his visit.

'I'm sorry, Mr Merrill. I . . . '

'No really don't apologise. I asked a question and you have answered. I always admire that. After this revolution you believe must come . . . Must come or may come?'

'Must come.'

'After it, do you believe that what we call evil will be abolished?'

'I don't believe in evil' Daniel said. 'That's metaphysics. Metaphysics is always class conflict in fancy dress.'

Alfred Merrill walked across to the window and looked down on the street. He spoke very low so that Daniel had to stand up and walk over towards the window to hear.

'I would like to recount a little story to you Daniel, then I really must let you go.

'I once handled a case in which a man, enraged beyond endurance by some force he believed was active inside him, lifted up his two year old son by the feet and swung his head against a wall until his skull was smashed and his brains were on the carpet. And in what was meant to be the briefing for his defence he simply kept repeating over and over again: "I don't know what possessed me."

'What do you think possessed him, Daniel, to execute so brutally his own little boy? What power could have pressed him into service? How precisely do you describe that in the language of your belief? In the language of Marx and Lenin and Stalin?'

Mr Merrill walked over to the scriptoire and took out his cheque-book. He handed Daniel the envelope after he had finished.

'Tell Claire there's really no further need for her to visit once a month. In future it shall be arranged that her account be credited automatically.'

The two men smiled bleakly at each other.

'Maybe you should ask her to marry you again Daniel.'

'She says she has married the revolution.'

'Then hers will be a very brutal home.'

❖   ❖   ❖

Aubrey Innis breathed in deeply. The open window of the Fowey Hotel gave him a fine view of the estuary and the morning was a bright one. Behind him on his table lay work-papers and a few books of reference. Smithson-Lowe was right. The book he had been forming for so long was now beginning to take final shape, though he still could not say exactly what that shape might be. But leaving London to come here was the beginning. From the window he could see the exact spot where local tradition held that Joseph of Arimathea had landed, accompanied by the youthful Jesus, to trade with the local tin-miners. And did those feet in ancient time . . . ?

Aubrey wondered how Joseph had first met the child. Perhaps he had been in the temple when the boy astonished the rabbis by preaching with an authority unknown before in one so young. Later after the unthinkable had happened on the hill of Calvary Joseph would return here bearing the cup Christ consecrated at the last supper, the cup which some say he held up to the body tortured on the cross to catch the sacred blood. East of here, exhausted, he planted his staff which flourished as the Glastonbury Thorn, blossoming at Christmas time.

He started to write:

Merlin
Chapter One
Leland's Journey

How gather the world into words? And with or without the world's acquiescence?

As long as they remain merely lists and inventories, they gleam on in innocence, these words. Shining miscellanies for acquiring or dispensing, like herbals or litanies of hours. But once let syntax enter and innocence must leave. Now either the words shall conform themselves to the world or the world to the words. The dreamers tell us they can live in a state of equivalence, one to another. But how?

To the antiquary the past is dark but all that emerges from it glitters, burnished by the brightness of his own vision. And how could he ever have stolen or stripped from their proper place these things rescued into the safe keeping of his knowledge? Such things were ordained to be his. When Leland was appointed to his post, a man was elevated to remove from oblivion the objects and documents of our creation; to place them under the sun of contemporary knowledge. Even if, in truth, his age like our own was a wound searching for a blade to clean it.

Such humanist and emblematic figures have vanished now into the obscurity of their own past. Now the kingdom has devolved on those for whom the sun's disc stands at twelve noon forever in the fullness of time. All shadows obliterated finally by reason. The past and the present having become the enemy, the future about to be constructed receives all their love. If time is the theatre of progress, then the disc spins one way only.

But Arthur lies still in his underground cave. There with his knights he watches roots grow, counting their inches in years as his sleep deepens into prescience, the life of action behind him dispersing like dawn mist. Now at last the shape of things to come grows lucid . . .

There was a knock at the door as Mrs Jenkyns brought in the London dailies and a pot of tea. He glanced at the front pages of the *Express* and the *Mail*, riffled quickly through *The Times* and then turned with curiosity to the middle pages of the *Daily Watchword* to find out what exactly Smithson-Lowe had done with his column. When the page fell open before him he looked at it for a moment before standing up and walking over to the window again. He breathed deeply a few times then walked back to read carefully the words before him.

For the first time what had come to be called the Innis Column was spread over two pages. And the banner now read, 'Aubrey Innis with Bobbie Morrell: The Start of a New Profile Series. Today: The Modern Artist.' The line sketch of himself, made many years before, had now crept to the far left-hand corner, while over to the right appeared a smilingly glamorous picture of Bobbie. And for the first time the column contained photographs. Aubrey read on:

What is a modern artist? Many of our readers have probably asked themselves this question at one time or another. After all most of us know what an artist is. Put us in front of a religious scene by Rembrandt, a portrait by Gainsborough or a landscape by Constable and we are perfectly at home. Here is skill matched with intelligence engaged in the production of beautiful form. These are the reproductions that most likely hang on our walls – their value does not diminish as the years pass.

But now take a look at the modern artists we are asked to admire. Picasso. Braque. Matisse. Fauvists and Cubists and Surrealists. What are they up to really? When we look at their canvasses, at the deformities and amputations said to represent the human form, at the uncontrolled splodges of colour said to describe a landscape, what on earth are we meant to make of it all?

There's always the smart set of course, smiling their superior smiles in London apartments. For them our failure to grasp these monuments to the modern is indicative of the smallness of our minds, or the narrowness of our morals. We seem to lack that Parisian breadth of character which permits a civilised guffaw every time the word marriage is mentioned.

Today we're going to look in a little more detail at what the word modern really means when applied to art and artists.

The two photographs shown on these pages (a new feature of the re-launched column!) portray the same person, though it may be hard to believe. Marianne Morris in 1914 was a classic English beauty. A highly educated young woman, she had been employed for some years as a director of the prestigious Smithson-Lowe gallery in Cork Street – owned by the proprietor of this very newspaper.

Some time that year Marianne went to Paris and became the mistress of Lucio Rovida – revered today as one of the heroes of the 'modern experiment'. The tragic results can be seen in the photograph we reproduce on the right-hand page. After fathering an illegitimate child upon her, Rovida died from drugs and drink and left Marianne to the life of degradation she all too clearly now conducts.

Far be it from us to challenge the intellectual credentials of so great a figure as George Bernard Shaw, but have we not the right to expect our artists to show at least a grain of human decency?

Aubrey stopped reading. He looked hard at the photograph of Marianne in the sordid tussle of her bed and he counted back the days since his lunch with Smithson-Lowe. He must have started work on all this the same day.

He stopped the car with Stonehenge in view but left the motor running. What's the point, he thought. He would be there with Bobbie already installed in her new post. He would remind him how much money he had been paid by the paper. He would probably mock the very conception of *Merlin* . . .

He turned the car around and started the drive back to Fowey. When he arrived at the hotel, he sat down at his table and wrote:

Dear Miss Morrell,
    Congratulations on joining me in the Innis column. As of now it is yours in its entirety. Your mind seems more in keeping with Mr Smithson-Lowe's present requirements.
    Sincerely, Aubrey Innis.

❖   ❖   ❖

Nathan Corinth's letter arrived at the hotel two weeks later, forwarded from the offices of the *Daily Watchword*. It was postmarked Berlin.

Dear Aubrey Innis,
    Met once didn't we? At Lowe's?
    You're Arthur's creature entirely now I see.
    I knew Rovida a little. A damaged man, doomed to self-destruct. Found himself in the vortex of the modern. Or lost

himself there. Another age would have served his talent better. He used the intelligence he had all the same, to travel a few leagues through the murk. What is your intelligence used for now? You've made yourself part of the soporific junkyard. You and the lickspittle versifiers whose muses are machines: Clio automated, Eros quantized into dialectics.

I don't know why I take the trouble to write. Yours being the sixth letter today and meanwhile I am paid nothing by anyone to write *Medea*. A cheque for fifty pounds from Wheeler and Wheeler every five years can't cover even my costs.

If you really want to know what the modern consists of why don't you come here – to Berlin. Herr Goebbels has just announced that this National Revolution has abolished 1789. Now that must be of interest surely? Even you must have noticed how democracy has confused our gullible peoples into believing they know something – and not a small thing but a great thing. Now we even have a league of nations with its silly bits of cotton and silk fluttering in the liberal wind.

Whatever the faults of the houses of religion (too many – far too many) at least they encouraged the good folk of Lilliput to chant and sing words hallowed and precise, not to blather ceaselessly in grunting swarms their own swineherd opinions!

Come here Innis if you're really tiring so much of the century. I myself have observed with wry amusement the little ceremonies around Unter den Linten and then the Reichstag firework display. What matter who torched it? To offer so much chatter as a holocaust, to cook so many spare tongues – perhaps at last 1789 *is* dying.

Last year – are you aware of this? – the USSR announced a five-year plan for the implementation of atheism. As though the soul were some new and variant potato. Make no mistake here. This is not the reckless Godlessness of Nietzsche with its sliced arteries and syphilitic splendours. This is grey statistic atheism by decree. Which way are you going Innis? And remember: One law for the lion & ox is oppression.

N

Corinth

CHAPTER FOUR

Large Causes, Smaller Deaths: 1936

Aubrey spent some time in the London Library following back the clues regarding Merlin and John Leland. Leland became ever more problematical the more he found out about him. Did he save something at least from the monastic libraries as they tumbled down beneath the watchful and possessive eye of Henry VIII? He never finished the work he had set out to do with his monarch's permission. Instead he went lengthily and unpleasantly insane. And his own fierce insistence on the literal truth of the Arthurian tales was to be subverted by the very techniques he himself espoused – travelling about and carefully looking.

At least with regard to the travelling about, Aubrey could follow, at vastly greater speed. His Bentley became the one constant factor in his life. More and more often now he would rise early. Sometimes he would sit for half an hour or so at his desk sketching out possible structures for *Merlin*, for his problem there was merely one of structure – once he had resolved that, the rest of it would fall into place, he was sure. But he never spent more than half an hour at this. Then he would gather his leather coat and hat and be down the steps, out to the special garage he had had specially built to house his car.

If he headed south east he could cross the North Downs and stop for lunch at Whitstable or Herne Bay. South would take him to Brighton where he sometimes stayed overnight if the weather was fine. But more and more often he headed west to Oxford. It was a soothing drive through the wooded roads and when he arrived he would park the car and then spend an hour or so in the Ashmolean. Occasionally he would make his way up to the reading room of the Bodleian and look at one of the rare early copies of the *Historia Regum Britanniae* or follow some elusive reference to Merlin. Then back out on the streets again and into the pubs. Few people recognised him, but whenever he returned to his car there would always be a group of under-graduates standing around it, smoothing their hands admiringly along its bonnet.

He had taken to calling in at The Boar's Head at Gerrard's Cross on his homeward journey. They had come to know him. Some of the local young women who drank in there even took bets on who would be the first to be given a ride in his Bentley.

On this particular evening the only solitary female drinker was Lindsay Cragge. The publican did not approve of her. As he put it to his wife, Since she looks like a tart and dresses like a tart and talks like a tart, I've a fair suspicion she may well be a tart. Lowering the tone of the place. The publican's wife said nothing, for she rather liked her and enjoyed her raucous gossip.

Aubrey parked up on the forecourt and ordered a pint of beer.

'Is that the rich one who worked for the papers?'

'That's him. In here every week or so.'

'What happened to his face?'

'It was during the war apparently. He was leading an attack – so they say.'

Lindsay looked over at Aubrey and continued looking until his eye caught hers. She gave him a smile of frank invitation. The publican's description of Lindsay was in fact accurate, as Lindsay herself would have been the first to concede. Lindsay knew only too well what men wanted. She also knew that they did not want it for very long. The impressive rapidity with which she bedded her employers had not yet led to a lengthy stay in any of her posts.

'Can I buy you a drink?' Aubrey asked as he smiled his crooked smile.

'Well that's very nice of you sir. I'll have a gin and it.'
'Large one?'
'Go on then.'

They were cruising down the road at about 40. Lindsay had never been in a car like this before and found it hard to believe it could go as fast as Innis claimed. There were still some things she was trying to establish.

'Her ladyship got a headache this evening has she?'

It took Aubrey a couple of seconds to catch up with her.

'Oh . . . there is no ladyship. No . . . lady.'

'Why not?'

'Perhaps I drive them all away.'

'Well you're certainly driving me away. How far are we going?'

'How far do you want to go?'

'All the way if there's no ladyship.'

Lindsay was wearing a tight black skirt which had a slit running up its right hand side. She gently manoeuvred herself on the seat next to him until the top of her stocking was showing. The arousal of men she regarded as a purely technical affair. She could do it while proceeding with a different train of thought entirely.

'You work for the papers don't you?'

'I used to work for the papers.'

'So what do you do now then?'

'I'm just finishing my book.'

'Oh a book! What's it about?'

'Merlin.'

'The magician?'

'The same.'

'It's a children's book then?'

Aubrey suddenly found the company he was keeping tiresome. He turned to look at Lindsay, thinking he would turn around now and drive her back to Gerrard's Cross. Lindsay raised her right leg a little higher and the white flesh above her stocking-top was clearly visible. He realised he wanted her. At least he wanted something which happened to be coincident with her body. He pressed a little harder on the accelerator. They could be at his house in twenty minutes.

'No it's not a children's book. It's a religious work really. You see Merlin is the presiding spirit of these islands, though he is imprisoned through sorcery. Through his own magic that he gave away, because he couldn't resist Vivienne, though he knew very well what she was.'

'And what was she?'

'No better than she should have been.'

Lindsay placed her hand at the top of Aubrey's thigh.

'Merlin was born from an incubus. He was part of the devil's scheme for the corruption of the world, but the scheme was thwarted by a single act of goodness. By a blessing.

'He brings Arthur into being, he makes Camelot possible. But he can't reverse the waywardness of men. He has to watch as the fellowship is destroyed. By lust.'

'I didn't understand a word of that' Lindsay said happily, probing a little further with her forefinger.

He had given her another gin and gone upstairs to make sure his bedroom had been reconstituted. When he came back down she was carefully examining the framed photographs on the table.

'The only thing I don't understand' she said as she walked over to him 'is where the pictures of the hero are.'

She put down her glass and pressed against him. Her hand squeezed between his legs and Aubrey's found the slit in her skirt.

'The hero?'

'The pictures of you in the war. You were a major weren't you. Led a famous attack. That's how they did for your face.'

It all stopped. Whatever had been ticking on or moving forward or rising in him, stopped. He turned away from her and was aware suddenly of the pungency of her perfume. And its cheapness.

'No, I spent the war in Aldershot and Dover and Boulogne and bloody Calais arranging supplies so the others could do the shooting. And my face got to look the way it is because three gentlemen objected to my driving a bus during the general strike and kicked it in. And I think perhaps Lindsay it's time you went back to Gerrard's Cross.'

Aubrey took a ten pound note from his pocket and held it out towards her.

'I don't take money for it. Some do but I don't. You can give me another drink though.'

She held her glass out towards him. He took it without meeting her eyes. She saw that she'd lost him. She'd seen this before with them, how one word out of place that knocked their precious pride an inch or two could halt them completely. One minute they were pawing at you, fighting through your clothes. Then nothing. A hole you both fell through. She didn't like failing.

'I'll go out and get you a cab' Aubrey was saying. 'Don't worry I'll pay him.'

'No' she said 'you'll take me back. I left in your car and I'm going back in it. You'll take me back to The Boar's Head. I want them to see me come back in with you. Do you understand?'

Aubrey closed his eyes in weariness.

'Then finish your drink and we can just get there by closing time.'

He drove hard and she talked intermittently. As much to herself as him.

'Fancied a bit of rough did we? A quick poke with the lower orders. With your fancy car and your stupid book. Probably a nancy boy, a kiss-me-Hardy seeing what it's like with a grown-up girl. Couldn't even get it up.'

'Shut up will you? Please shut up.'

As he pulled into the forecourt, she turned to him.

'Now you're coming in with me and you're going to have a drink. And you keep a nice smile stuck all over that corkscrew face of yours. Like a little boy who's finally found out where you're supposed to put it. I have my reputation to think of.'

Aubrey drank three large scotches in swift succession while Lindsay whispered among her friends.

'He might be rolling in money but I can tell you girls you'll go home a lot happier after a session with Albert over there. Still it's worth it, just for a ride in his car. And he does have a beautiful house.

'I believe that I'm owed some money from our little bet?'

They all groaned and started to rummage in their bags.

And Aubrey made his escape.

The specifications of the car stated its top speed as 92. It was a dark section of the road when Aubrey hit it, still cursing to himself into the wind.

The little Morris coming the other way was travelling at 25 miles per hour. All Jack English saw was a smear of headlights before he swerved. It was unfortunate that the side of the road fell away so steeply. Otherwise it is possible that he and his young wife would have lived.

Aubrey did not stop.

❖   ❖   ❖

The story was picked up by the papers in the evening editions the following day. The *Watchword* carried it the day after. The little boy of five who was orphaned caught a little of the public imagination. It was not however front page material.

The *Watchword* was in any case feverishly preparing for its yearly celebration that very evening. At the Ritz, where they went every year.

The people were getting drunk in three distinct layers. The bottom rung, typesetters, printmen, runners, junior reporters simply downed the most potent liquor they could get their hands on as swiftly as possible. They then made highly-publicised passes at the women nearest to them on their allotted tables, who received it all with good humour. The middle rank, department managers, established reporters, columnists, were more acid and reserved, pacing themselves a little self-consciously while smiling sourly at the antics of their under-lings. At the very top table, Arthur Smithson-Lowe's select circle gave the impression that they were not drinking at all, though full bottles kept being delivered and empty ones removed.

The tradition had now been set for ten years: two hours of merriment, then the boss's address, characterised by his poison-ous wit. After that, mayhem.

He rose at eight-thirty precisely. Silence immediately fell. As he tapped his glass for formality's sake, the little man was led from behind the screen where he had been waiting. He joined Smithson-Lowe on the podium. There was an incredulous muttering from below, for Smithson-Lowe, immaculately rounded in his evening jacket, now laid an arm around the shoulder of this bedraggled dirty down-and-out, his tattered shirt hanging over his trousers.

'Ladies and gentlemen, it is my great pleasure this evening to be able finally to introduce you to the single most important patron of the *Watchword*.'

He waited as his words registered through the drink and more muttering ensued.

'It is to this gentleman before you that we all owe our existence. He is the man with the golden bough. He can take us lower than we ever thought possible.

'He looks a little battered at the moment it's true but then the last few years have not been kind to him. Work has been hard to find and he has lost his self-confidence. But don't be taken in by his hang-dog look – he's very resourceful. A good bath, a change of clothes, a few decent meals and a promise of a decent wage at the end of the week and this little fellow will be ready to build you another empire.

'You should see him at work. No really – you think I'm being ironic but it's not so. Watch him rivetting and welding. See the boats growing till they tower over his own somewhat humble home. Why he can build racing cars, towers, hospitals, ocean liners, back-to-back houses, mansions, tables, chairs, aeroplanes. He's a very talented individual.

'And what of his tastes? This is interesting because when I launched this great enterprise of ours, this *Daily Watchword* we are all so proud to be involved in . . . '

Applause rose from the audience and Smithson-Lowe bowed gravely to acknowledge it.

' . . . as I say, when our newspaper was first shaped in the womb of the times, I thought I had to follow him. I watched his every move. I scrutinised him for the mildest gesture. It took a while for me to understand that when you gaze into the void, it is only your own features that return your gaze.

'We fill him up, you see. Otherwise he must remain empty. The church once filled him. Wars and crusades filled him, but now the poor little sod's empty. So we fill him. And he likes to be shocked. Give him a frisson, then lots of graphic detail. What the rich do in their beds is always a dead certainty. The results of hideous violence – domestic, international, vehicular. Any form of carnage, cruelty. Anything that's foreign to his little world – and almost everything is – can be treated with contempt and he will applaud.

'I call him common denominator, but you can call him what you like, he'll almost certainly answer. Heart of oak, prole, soldier of the Lord, Mr Average, Mr Medium Malicious, Jack Faultless, Comrade What's-His-Name. He could tell you heartrending stories, make no mistake about it, bless his little heart. Of grandad's labours down the pit, his sister croaking in childbirth for want of the price of a nurse. But big words stick in his gullet so don't get too grand with him. Keep informing him that the rich are worse than he is, that foreigners are nastier and weaker, and that everything will shortly be all right.

'And never forget, he pays your wages. This is the demeanour I expect you to adopt before him.'

Smithson-Lowe took his political zero by the shoulders and kissed him ceremoniously on both cheeks. Then, with a rapidity that brought a gasp from his audience, he rammed his fist into the man's stomach – considerably harder than at the rehearsal.

As the actor was helped out of the room and given his thirty five pounds, he was swearing quietly at Arthur Smithson-Lowe.

The publisher had sat down and closed his eyes. The vicious pain in his head had intensified and the numbness through the left of his body was spreading. He drained his glass of whisky and cursed himself for a fool.

At the back of the hall, Bobbie Morrell was swaying drunkenly and spilling her drink. As Lucky Morris approached her, dressed most elegantly in his evening jacket and white bow-tie, she called to him.

'Well, Lucky, you do look . . . impressive. Well, positively delicious actually.'

'Well thank you Bobbie. You look quite a sight yourself.'

'Arthur is obviously happy with your organising skills. You do organise things for him don't you?'

'I do indeed. Parties and displays. I arrange for services to be provided.'

'Yes I've heard about some of them. You're obviously very resourceful, Lucky. I hope it doesn't get into the papers.'

She laughed at her own joke, but Lucky didn't. He seldom laughed.

'But my my, Lucky, you are so . . . fetching in that outfit. I can hardly believe it's the little boy I met in Wandsworth.'

Bobbie had wrapped her arm around the base of his spine and her hand was sliding lower.

'And you're so . . . trim too. Would you like to come back to my flat after the party? It has a lovely view over the park.'

'No thanks Bobbie.'

'You little ingrate. After all I've done for you. Don't you find me attractive then?'

Bobbie pouted in mock despair.

'You're a very attractive woman Bobbie – we all know that. After all you wouldn't be where you are today if you weren't. Would you Bobbie?'

'So why not come back then when I ask you? You could do something normal for a change instead of setting up Babylonish spectacles for old Arthur.'

'You're very gracious Bobbie. But you must excuse me all the same. It's just I'm rather anxious to make sure I don't get what Arthur's got. I'm handing out rather a lot of these at the moment.'

He took from the inside pocket of his jacket a card which bore the name of a Harley Street specialist and handed it to Bobbie.

'You have an appointment for Monday morning. Nine o'clock. Good luck.'

❖   ❖   ❖

The first time he had paid her, it had placed her in Lucio Rovida's bed. The second time was in recompense for her public humiliation in the pages of his newspaper. Now Arthur Smithson-Lowe was paying her son. For what? she had shouted at him when he came home and told her. What is he paying you for?

'To amuse him mother. That's what he pays everyone for – or hadn't you noticed?'

She had slapped Lucio across the face then. Hard. And had never seen him since.

Now she saw Smithson-Lowe everywhere. He owned the streets. He owned the shops with their papers and pictures. He owned the people. She could see the way they grinned and turned away from her, whispering filth. She could no longer find the edge where Smithson-Lowe's power ceased. One night, under the railway arch where she sometimes slept in case his men were waiting for her back at the flat, she saw that he had planned everything. He had sent her to Paris, anticipating her failure at painting and her rendezvous with Rovida. He needed a boy and had arranged for her to provide one.

The two notes she had sent him, warning him of the retribution to come, she had made sure were untraceable by typing them on the old Remington at an office where she had a job – though not for long.

It was while searching for a place where the assassination might take place – Fleet Street was too obvious and too dangerous – that she first heard the singing. It was the curious tranquillity of the sound which drew her in. There was nothing rational about her choice. She wanted to be inside that music. And that is how she found herself inside the Jesuit church in Farm Street for the first time.

After that she simply kept going. And when she knocked on the door of the presbytery, that was through no rational process either. She wanted to be deeper inside those ceremonies than she could be now.

'In short you want to find peace' said Father Ignatius Tyrrel and smiled.

Marianne had been fortunate that he had been in attendance that day. Some of the other priests were of a distinctly less sympathetic demeanour. But the many tragedies in Father Tyrrell's own life had edged him into gentle wisdom. He was the least judgemental of men. He knew that when the Good Lord said, Judgement is mine, He meant it, and he often cringed to hear his colleagues taking upon their own sinful selves the role of judge. 'Judge not lest ye be judged, father' he remonstrated, 'the task assigned us is the dispensing of mercy.' But they took little notice.

He listened patiently to Marianne's sorry tale. As she admitted everything to him she felt the burden shift. He performed over a number of months the formalities necessary to receive her into the church. And then the real conversation began between them, until at last it all seemed to flow together and she could no longer remember the separate occasions on which the words had been spoken.

'When we first come to make our act of confession, both to ourselves and to God, we often think of ourselves as uniquely sinful – which from our own vantage point of course, we are. We know our own sin far better than we can ever know another's. What you have realised though, realised it by the very fact of coming here, is that you are not damned. You may have felt damned many times in your life, but you are not. You have entered now the community of forgiveness. These rituals are not here for their own sake – never make that mistake – they are the traces of God's action in history . . . They are the runes by which we trace the eternal.

'He has never ceased to be active, remember. Indeed He is active with the enactment of every sacrament. Like that of penance, which is now going to absolve you of all your sins. You will be fresh in the world again. Though fallen, of course, we must never forget. Our own flesh will not let us forget. Nothing spontaneously innocent is available to us. We have made that impossible by our sin, which thing of darkness we must acknowledge ours. Once we have taken responsibility for our sin, then we may be absolved from it.

'You must never again think of yourself as worthless. That is a grave sin and, if I may say so, the gravest of the Protestant heresies. The works of man may still shine in the darkness if man himself submits to the scheme of redemption.

'The flames of hell are but the flames of truth. No more than that. And hell's agonies which so much ink and paint has been spilt over are merely the free resistance of an independent creature to that truth. If this is punishment, it is self-induced and self-maintained. You must leave damnation alone now, leave that to His mercy. Think of what we mean by the new creation.

'You see, whatever might evolve in this world, the soul does not evolve. The world starts anew with each fresh birth. Our belief is merely the remembrance of that fact. You must start to pray now, each day, for it is prayer that makes us vulnerable to God's possibilities. You of all people must know the truth of how Dostoevsky described the choice before the modern age: either Christ luminous in the mandorla or man encased in his machine – well, something like that anyway. We live in the age of parody. The reading of the newspaper parodies the reading of the daily office. Go to a cinema. See those faces raised up out of the darkness. They certainly appear worshipful. But I do wonder if truth can be rendered down like that to celluloid, with those shapes merely going through the motions . . .

'I am digressing. The younger priests tell me that is my besetting sin. "Father Tyrrell" they say "you have meandered again".'

Marianne remembered smiling for the first time that day. The old man looked at her and closed his eyes.

'Your penance, Marianne, is not one that can be accomplished in twenty minutes sitting at the back of a church.

'Your penance is to learn to forgive Arthur Smithson-Lowe.'

✧   ✧   ✧

1936 was as good a time as any to consider how the young Einstein had tried to envisage what it would be like to ride on a ray of light. You might be travelling too swiftly for your own image ever to arrive in the mirror. At this speed then we could never acquire an image of ourselves. Fellow travellers would have to describe us, and we would have to believe their particular truths.

King George the Fifth might have been in a better position to comment on the accuracy of this now, since he had died in January. It is unlikely he would have thought much of the idea before that point. No truth was relative as far as he was concerned.

He had grown crabby and uncivil towards the end, though no royal prerogative was involved there. He was particularly infuriated with his son David, about to become the next king of England. His father thought he dressed like a cad, talked like a cad and, as he told the boy on numerous occasions, *was* a bloody cad. He will ruin himself within twelve months of my death, he remarked.

As soon as the king was dead, the new King Edward ordered that the clocks at Sandringham, which were always set a half hour ahead of Greenwich time, so as to provide more daylight for the shooting, should be set at the same time as all the other clocks in the kingdom. They were all ticking at the same tempo now.

At least King George had been treated in the year before his death to a jubilee. This relatively recent invention claimed the imprimatur of time immemorial. The bunting and the flags stretched from one coast to the other.

Orage would have detested it, but death had spared him the spectacle. Before he died he had been alienated entirely from Gurdjieff, a man who'd once prompted him to cross the Atlantic and for whom now he wouldn't even cross the street. He had come to see him as someone merely acquiring power while claiming to spread wisdom.

The *Daily Watchword* had referred to the jubilee as a 'welcome holiday from reality'. It was a phrase which Claire Merrill registered with profound irritation. For Claire did not believe in holidays: the annual parenthesis in the life sentence, she called them.

Daniel was determined to have one all the same. And what's more he was going to Blackpool. The nearest he had come to a holiday in three years was when he had taken a day off to travel up to the Eastleigh Aerodrome in Southampton. He'd gone there to see the Vickers' Spitfire, and to gaze astonished into its 12-cylinder liquid-cooled engine, made by Rolls-Royce. They'd given it the name of Merlin.

But Daniel was tired, exhausted, all-in. Hitler was in the Rhineland, Mussolini was staying in Abyssinia, and Daniel had a nasty premonition that the fascists in Spain were going to prove more troublesome than some of his comrades seemed to think. Anyway, he wanted a holiday. And a holiday meant Blackpool, whatever Claire's sneers or snarls to the contrary.

They could have driven up of course. He would have liked that. If only Claire had agreed upon the purchase of the perfectly-maintained Morris he'd found after keeping his eyes open for it over the years.

'I find it astonishing Dan, you don't see how it is the ultimate form of bourgeois transport. The workers don't drive round in cars in the Soviet Union. It is a tiny artificial unit. A train will carry four hundred people at a time. This carries one or two, its fuel shipped thousands of miles from the Persian Gulf. A long chain of expropriated workers all the way.'

Daniel would have liked that Morris all the same.

And he was going to have his holiday in Blackpool. In a lodging-house, for a week. He wanted his food made for him. Claire didn't cook much and it seemed to Daniel that he had been hungry pretty much ever since they'd met. At least she'd given up the vegetarianism she practised when they'd first cohabited. In his first week in her house he could find nothing but lettuces and nettles. He'd very nearly eaten one of the cats.

They went on the train. Third class. Claire was nervous, more so as they approached their destination. Daniel picked it up and started smiling, increasingly confident.

Mrs Trevelyan's lodging house was a few streets down from the central pier. They put their suitcase in the bedroom there and Claire looked about her, dispirited.

'There's no bathroom here then, Dan?'

'There's a toilet one floor down and a bath one floor up. There's a special charge for using the bath. And you have to book it. People don't normally bother unless they have an accident with the tar. It melts in the heat.'

'And the meals?'

'Downstairs in the meal room. Everybody eats there. Now I'm going to take you out to see the pier and the golden mile. And I'm going to have a decent pint. Northern bitter. The good Lord knows I deserve it after all these years of exile.

'And Claire, will you for Christ's sake try to put a smile on your bloody face. This is where we take our pleasure.'

They left their lodgings and on the way out Mrs Brown stated, smilingly firm, that tea would be at five. Sharp.

'When's dinner then?' Claire asked.

'That is dinner.'

'But she said tea.'

'Tea is dinner. Well, it isn't, to be fair. Dinner's in the middle of the day. At lunchtime. This is the north. It's not like blokes down south working in offices. A working man – doing real work, mind – needs something to sustain him in the middle of the day. So that's when we have our dinner. Then come five we have our tea.'

'And then?'

'Supper. If you're still peckish at nine.'

They were at the pier and Daniel was buying the tickets to get through the turnstile. He could smell the sea and he was happy.

They walked up and down the pier. Daniel stopped at every stall where a man was selling his gimcrack devices, his card packs for cheating, or his farting cushions. He stopped to look at a curtain of dirty postcards and chortled happily as he read them. Claire kept looking at his face and tried to remind herself that she did know this man well.

It was around three as they came off the pier.

'Come on. Up that way there's a pub I remember. If it's still there. Must be. The government could never close down pubs. Then there really would be a revolution. Blackpool is one of the few places in Great Britain where you can drink for twenty four hours a day if you know where to go.'

Daniel grabbed Claire by the hand and started to run across the tramlines. The gesture did not make her entirely happy.

Inside the Singing Whistle he bought himself a pint and Claire a large gin and tonic.

'There' he said, clinking his glass against hers, 'like old times.'

'Is it?' Claire said vacantly.

'Now don't tell me you've forgotten. After that meeting during the strike, when you set your cap at me, you drank gin and I drank beer.'

'I never . . . I never set my cap at you . . . that's a very vulgar expression.'

'You sat down at my table and let me buy you drinks. And later that night you took me into your bed. If that's not setting your cap at a fellow, then I don't know what is.'

Claire did not like this. Things were suddenly out of her control. She watched Daniel down his pint and walk across to the bar to get another, a broad smile on his face.

She chivvied him out of the place at five minutes to five, after his fourth pint.

As they hurried back towards the lodging house, he stopped and turned her round towards him.

'This is what they want, you know. They don't want opera and Shakespeare and walks in the country. They certainly don't want Lenin on nationalism or Stalin on the language question. And they quite definitely don't want our own precious Comrade Smart lecturing them about what they should and shouldn't be doing. And his interest in you, if you don't mind my saying so, has as much to do with the contents of your knickers as your grasp of revolutionary theory, comrade. If there were a revolution tomorrow and the working class of this country could decide their own fate, this is what they would want. This is what they like. And for this week I'm going to like it too.

'Now why don't you take that sour middle-class look of disapproval off your face and enjoy it as well? Otherwise Claire I'm going to have to report you to the party for inadequate proletarian credentials.'

They arrived at the lodging house at three minutes past five.

The meal room was full. It was also silent except for the clinking of soup spoons against soup bowls. There would be a periodic whisper from a child, promptly shushed back into silence by an adult.

Claire and Daniel's place was laid for them, but there was no soup bowl and no soup spoons. They sat down. After a couple of minutes Claire said,

'Where's the soup?'

The old lady next to them leaned over to her confidentially and said,

'She put it out and took it away.'

Claire stared at her, looking for signs, trying to find her way in this new situation.

'To keep it warm?'

'No love. You see, if you're not at your table at five dead on, they put your food out then take it away again. It keeps everybody honest. Been drinking have you both? I can smell it on your breath. Mrs Trevelyan doesn't like that either. Says if folks need to sup ale they can do it during the hours of darkness so she needn't catch sight of their faces.'

Whatever anger had been rising in Claire during the course of the day now took focus.

'Go tell her we want our soup Dan.'

'You tell her' Daniel said. A false move, he recognised immediately.

Claire stomped out of the room and down the corridor towards the serving hatch. She was now out of earshot of the rest of the boarders. They looked at each other and at Daniel with a look the righteous might display a few seconds after the commencement of Armaggedon. Then she was back.

'Get up Dan, we're going.'

'Look, let me talk to them – I'll sort it out. I'm from the north, I'll . . .'

'You'll not do anything. We're going. Now come on.'

They walked and she explained. He's booked you in as Mr and Mrs Miskin, she had said, but I can see you're not. No wedding ring. I don't actually approve of people who live over the brush coming here and using my house for it. It's a respectable house, this. And those sheets are expensive to launder. They weren't going back there, she said. If he went back there, then he was going alone. They ate fish and chips. Then they went to Yates' Wine Lodge and drank.

Unexpectedly, Claire was enjoying herself.

'Get me another drink, Dan, and this time make it a decent size.'

He did as he was told but wondered whatever would happen to them later. At least Claire had her bag round her shoulder. There always seemed to be some reserves of money in that. Anyway, he'd now had so much beer he wasn't sure he greatly cared.

Outside under the stars they walked along the promenade. She linked her arm through his.

'Lodging houses are bourgeois' she said.

'No they're not' he said. 'They're working class.'

'Well, the need for them's bourgeois. They constitute a false sense of security.'

'They constitute a way of keeping warm and sleeping in a bed.'

'I don't want to sleep in a bed tonight. I'm feeling reckless, Dan, it's all that drink you've poured inside me. It's just like the first time. Remember?'

Daniel certainly remembered. He often thought about that axis about which his life had swung.

'If we're not going to sleep in a bed love, then where are we going to sleep?'

'You told me how you hid in the toilet of the train when you were younger, and slept on the dunes.'

'I was fourteen.'

'And now you're forty three and I'm forty. And we're going to sleep there again.'

'It gets very cold.'

'Well then, you're going to have to warm me up, aren't you Dan? Just like you used to in the beginning. Isn't it about time the proletariat tried a little harder to get on top of the bourgeoisie?'

They walked down hand in hand beyond the south pier and they found the most sheltered spot they could in the sand-dunes. Then they made love for the first time in over a year. And when Daniel woke up the following morning, hungover, cold and grubby, Claire had vanished.

He walked up and down in the sand and then on the promenade looking for her. But an instinct told him she was gone. He went back to the boarding-house to get his suit-case.

Mrs Trevelyan was out shopping. Her daughter Beth took him up to the room.

'Where's your lady friend then?'

'My wife' he said, the irritation in his voice unconcealed.

'She's not your wife love. I've seen plenty of wives. I know what wives are like. She's nobody's wife, that one.'

Something in the frankess of the observation, in the old familiar intonations he remembered well, combined with his unacknowledged fury at Claire – to have awoken that in him which they'd both agreed to register deceased for the sake of the revolution – made Daniel sit down on the bed and weep.

Beth walked over to him and ruffled his hair with her fingers.

'You smell' she said.

'Go have a bath before mother comes back and you won't get charged. And when you come out I'll give you some tea.'

Daniel did as he was told. Afterwards he had his tea. Then he slipped into the sharp linen sheets and slept.

He stayed the week. Peace settled between himself and his landlady. Now the hoity-toity bitch is gone, as she put it to her daughter, I've no grouse with him. Quite a nice sort of bloke by himself.

Mrs Trevelyan did not know that Beth, setting out for her evening constitutional each day at seven thirty, was met by Daniel underneath the central pier. They walked together and talked. Daniel told her the story of his life, with only certain parts censored. It started to make sense to him for the first time as he put it into words.

Beth was plumply attractive in a manner the Victorians approved and painted. Her shape was out of fashion now, but that made her in Daniel's eyes all the more desirable. Her smile was a statement of fact – he had forgotten what it was like to be with women like this. Assuming he had ever known.

Only once, with a beer too many inside him, did he manhandle her, pressing himself against her with some urgency. She seemed unperplexed.

'I like you Daniel' she said, 'and I would marry you if you asked me. But you're a lot older than me, and I think you're very confused. Though a lot more interesting than the boys I've met here. If you got rid of your grand friend, then you could have me. But not for nothing.'

Here suddenly, as though she had crossed the threshold of a home, her own, presided over by Eros as though it were a household god, she took his hand and placed it gently inside her blouse.

'I'd make you happy, you know. She could never make anybody happy. I saw her eyes and I know. I reckon you've always been down in the dunes with her, did you but know it. Getting dirty and cold.'

Daniel arrived back at Primrose Hill confused. Did he want to marry Beth, soft, welcoming Beth? The hard and bony dissatisfaction of his present mate had overstayed its welcome. But the only home he had to live in belonged to her. And he didn't have any money. He was starting to perceive the shape of his problem . . .

The house on Primrose Hill was dark. He walked though all

the rooms, with a growing sense of something altered. Then he found the note on the table:

'Alf had to back out of the Moscow trip. I've taken his place. The land of the future at last. See you in a few weeks. Sorry to leave you in the sand like that. I'm sure there's a scientific explanation for me, but someone's forgotten to publish it.'

The next day the telegram came.

Inconvenient I have no doubt. But I appear to be dying with unanticipated speed. You are my only child, Claire. Please come.   *Father.*

❖   ❖   ❖

Nathan Corinth dreamed a window of naked mannikins saluting. The children turned up in the dark from different parts of the city and formed a line before the shop. Then at a single call from a figure hidden in a doorway, they threw their stones and the glass smashed. They pulled the mannikins out into the puddles in the street. They broke off their arms and legs and conducted mock sword fights with them. All around them lay the sodden and dirty flags from the last celebration.

He woke. It was dawn. He lifted the sheet so he could better examine his signora. She slept still, lightly snoring. She was ten years his senior and her body had thickened with childbearing and hardship. She had been his landlady until he could no longer pay the rent.

The ageing enchantress, he thought. Perhaps this was what Jason had fled from. Her breasts hung slack against her, half-sapped from suckling.

He slipped from the bed and dressed quickly downstairs. His bag was small and already packed. He bore little from place to place. Of most importance was the newly-completed *Medea IV*, ready for delivery to Wheeler and Wheeler in London.

From the Via Cavallotti it would have been quicker to walk

over the Ponte della Vittoria to the station. But he wanted a last look at this city which he preferred to all others.

He made his way over the Ponte Vecchio and into the Piazza Della Signoria so he could stand and look at Perseus. It was Perseus that held him always. Cellini had captured something in the poise, with the head of Medusa held aloft, her ganglia still yearning for the body they were severed from. And the sickle sword held steady on the same latitude as his penis. Ready for the next adventure.

He caught the Paris train and from thence to Victoria, using the ticket provided for him by A.D.Carvely of Wheeler and Wheeler.

When he arrived at the offices in Museum Street, he had taken a detour from Victoria to see two of the latest films. Then next to him on the underground had sat a young woman, slickly and darkly suited, who opened an oval clasp and started to brush a bruise of blue powder onto her eyelid. She caught his eyes as they swerved across the mirror. He turned then and looked her full in the face and she turned back immediately towards the dark of the tunnel. The musk of her perfume caught him.

They anoint themselves still for enchantment, he thought. But the force of it is sapped by urbanity. Not Medea.

When he arrived at his publisher's office, he opened his bag and dropped his manuscript onto the editor's table.

'Volume Four' he said and sat down in the one chair in the office that promised any comfort. He was still wearing his remarkably grubby overcoat, which came down to his feet.

'How are you Nathan?'

'Temporarily empty. And you?'

'Life continues. Tell me of the goings-on in Italy.'

'Oh, Muss hammers on, you know.'

'It's a nasty business in Germany at the moment.'

'This is from the British papers?'

'And some books. And a number of first-hand accounts . . . '

'I shouldn't necessarily believe any of it if I were you. I don't read the papers myself, as you know. I try to form my own judgements, free from the age's noisome idiom.'

'There are photographs, Nathan.'

'Photographs! Our ridiculous and photographic age. Our monocular times. You're a poet Carvely, how can you talk to me of photographs? How can any photograph ever tell the truth when a machine intervenes between mind and world? It is preposterous for a man with two eyes to look at pictures fashioned by a cyclopean monster with one. Photographs are the dead icons of the press.'

'All the same Nathan, I shouldn't underestimate the sheer unpleasantness of what is happening in Germany.'

'They are trying to undo a century and a half of history. Do you think that someone's not going to get a broken head?

'Every damned village in France has a statue of Robespierre sitting in the centre of it. Robespierre! The mob exonerator. Remember? He let them off, that's why they loved him. Until they killed him – it never takes long. Who's the last one they've just done for in Russia? No matter.

'Robespierre is where it starts, our dedicated lawyer on behalf of the poor. The defender of actors, Jews, negroes, slaves. The sea-green incorruptible, the steady beacon of the Committee of Public Safety. What was it he had made it his business to find again – *une volunté une*? Well that will was Medusa's snakes, writhing in Demos. They speak as one, they scream as one, they devour as one. It was our philanthropic lawyer who took terror from the gods and gave it to the state. And now Perseus must cut the bitch's head off. There's no gentler surgery will cure it.

'I've just seen two films – the latest products of this civilization we should presumably be defending against the Germans and Italians. *Modern Times* – have you seen it?'

Carvely shook his head.

'Little man lost in the machine that man has made. The perception behind it is trite, and the little fellow grins incessantly. But he never fights anyone. All the fights are ghost fights and no-one gets hurt. There's no Perseus to wield a sword, only this little fellow with his saboteur's grin. You remember the etymology? *Sabot, saboter.* They throw their wooden sandals into the machines. That way nobody gets hurt and history is reversed. There's no death, is there?

'The other film I saw was about a giant magpie-coloured mouse with an idiotic voice. And nothing at all can die in it, because whatever is broken is healed again by the cartoonist's hand. So it's immortality at last.

'Is this the culture you want to save?'

'There are other things in this culture – perhaps not so . . . advertised.'

'I do not share your faith Carvely, you know that. I still hear the voices of the old gods.'

'What will you do, Nathan?'

'A little writing for some periodicals probably. Continue the search for the goddess.'

'Take care, Nathan. Try to be a little more . . . politic.'

'It would be the first time.'

'It would indeed.'

❖   ❖   ❖

Claire did not enjoy the journey to Moscow. She had never got on well with the other members of the party, and they thought her too grand by half. Halfway across Europe, by an unspoken agreement, they decided to leave one another alone. So Claire continued with her reading. Her excitement grew all the same.

John Strachey had said it for all of them when he wrote in 1933, "To travel from the capitalist world into Soviet territory is to pass from death to birth." She was going to the land of the future. She was journeying to where history was made, not simply endured.

The picture of it in her mind was a mosaic, made up of all the photographs and all the films they had seen. Workers smiled on windy prairies, their tractors shining behind them. Factories hummed with the joy of production, once the exploitation had been taken out of it. Fresh faces pointing into the wind. The dialectics of laughter. Machines blessed by poetry and poetry by machines.

She had not expected the greyness that hovered somehow around the ochre buildings, nor the silence that seemed pervasive behind each spoken word. She had studied Russian for two years. She had a natural gift for languages and had learnt quickly. Daniel had been bitter about this, for he had to abandon his course, finding himself hopelessly ill-equipped to either pronounce or remember the words.

'There do appear to have been some advantages to your bourgois education then' he'd said crossly.

'Temper temper Dan' she had replied, 'from each according to his abilities, remember?'

The guide they were allocated infuriated her. She was in the process of explaining that the Moscow underground was the first in the world.

'Excuse me' Claire had said, 'but I think you'll find the one in London precedes it by the better part of a century.'

'This is not true. This is capitalist propaganda of the west.'

Claire switched to Russian and the guide's face hardened.

'This is not capitalist propaganda of the west, comrade. And in case you've missed it, I'll inform you once again: I am a member of the British Communist Party. I am the education officer for my branch. I am a Marxist-Leninist. But I don't remember either Marx or Lenin recommending deceit or ignorance as the way forward for socialism.'

Finally she simply escaped. Although it had been made plain to them on their arrival that it was strictly forbidden, she quietly packed her bag and slipped out onto the street one evening. She had tied her hair up like the Moscow women, and with her long dark coat she did not look at all conspicuous. Her Russian was heavily accented, but they looked at her with no greater suspicion than they did their own countrymen.

She found the little café with the music and she ordered vodka. This was not served there – not officially anyway. But a hand pulled her back to a table out of the light and a bottle appeared from out of an overcoat.

Claire had been right, in an odd sort of way, about one thing: it was a land of poetry. Stalin himself was a poet. Georgian children had learnt his verses by heart. He took a keen interest in all matters artistic. For example, he wished to be a tall man with strong hands, but Providence obliged him in neither respect. A number of his portrait painters, with a too-clumsy notion of socialist realism, were consequently shot.

After Mayakovsky's suicide in 1930 it seemed the muse came electrically alive and, after that, never even closed her eyes for sleep. She did need to be watchful though. In one six year stretch a quarter of the members of the Union of Writers lost their lives. Stalin and Beria between them ruled Helicon. Beria liked to shoot his writers personally. Stalin was more formal and more distant.

In 1934, having had Mandelstam arrested for a few cryptic but unflattering verses about him, Stalin telephoned Pasternak. The giant's breath on the telephone, intimate with menace. This was the man of steel, goading and questioning, querying one man's loyalty to a writer comrade – and of course his loyalty to the state. A breath blown from the monolith of that smile. The hand holding the receiver re-wrote the page of progress with each new pamphlet. Or simply tore it out.

'He is a master of his craft, you would presumably agree? You sound equivocal to me comrade. If I wielded a pen to make verses as you do I'd like to think I'd show more solidarity than this with others engaged in the same dangerous trade.

'I have some poetry here in front of me which suggests that all who survive the age are furriers, soft-shoe practitioners. I'd have thought the truth should be asked to come out loud and clear myself. There was a rhyme we used to learn at school . . . now what was it . . . about turning a bird's neck inside out to slipper your foot. Then killing a fulmar to squeeze the oil from it . . . to lay the troubled waters to rest . . . '

Vladimir Litvinov was reckless. His friends kept warning him to keep his mouth shut before the men in black cars turned up to close it permanently for him. He had made for Claire in the gloom of the café, and had soon established that she was English. Then she had told him that she was a communist.

He looked at her long and silently.

'Why have you come here?' he asked.

'To see the future being born' she said, a little unsurely.

'You'll have to wait then until they are finished murdering the past.'

Vladimir's friend kicked him under the table and looked at him with genuine alarm.

'My friend here warns me to be silent. He thinks you may be a spy. But I don't think so.

'If you want to understand this beautiful country, don't read Marx, don't read Engels, don't read Lenin and don't read the man of steel. Read Dostoevsky. Read abut Shigalyov. From infinite freedom he starts, and ends with infinite despotism. You know what Shigalyov recommended? That everyone must spy on everyone else. Because everyone belongs to everyone else, you see. You don't own your soul, it's not a piece of private property. You understand? All slaves, and all equal in slavery, that is what Shigalyov believes. You know what he said? "Cicero's tongue will be cut out, Copernicus will have his eyes gouged out, Shakespeare will be stoned." Slaves you see must always be equal.'

It caused a little diplomatic stir at the time. The British Communist Party received a reprimand from Moscow and was asked to review its admission procedure. But they couldn't find her. A few people had spotted her with a young man named Litvinov, a poet and a trouble-maker the authorities had been taking an interest in for a while. But they had gone. Disappeared somewhere. They would turn up, no-one doubted that.

✧   ✧   ✧

Daniel Miskin had to arrange hurriedly to acquire a passport, for he had never been out of the country before. He found his journey to the Swiss mountains difficult but exhilarating. In Switzerland itself he simply stared hour after hour through the train window. It had never occurred to him that anywhere in the world could actually look like this.

He arrived at the chalet towards evening. The nurse took his coat, and led him to the bedside. He was shocked by the old man's appearance. The skin on his face seemed blue, around his eyes the flesh was red. He seemed to be drawing breath from somewhere impossibly deep inside him.

Daniel sat down and took his hand. The eyes opened and a vestige of a smile appeared on the ravaged features. He gestured to be lifted up into a sitting position. Then he started to talk.

'Daniel, why have I come here to die? I knew the disease in my lungs was killing me, but I still listened to them. Doctors. I should have stayed home . . . Claire?'

'In the Soviet Union.'

'My God. Why?'

'A place came free on one of the Party's trips . . . It's something we've both wanted to do.'

'Yes of course. See the workshop where they're rebuilding reality?'

'Something like that.'

'So she doesn't know, my daughter?'

'No, Mr Merrill, she would have come, I don't doubt it.'

The old man squeezed Daniel's hand, a hand so frail now that Daniel stroked it.

'So it's just the two of us again. I'm going quickly now. Whatever the Swiss guard over there says to the contrary. I have

114

made some arrangements it is important you know about. On the table there is the card of Monsieur Laplage. His office is in the village at the bottom of the hill. He has all that is legally required to settle matters.

'I'm leaving everything to Claire and you, jointly.'

Daniel was surprised, too surprised to be pleased.

'Well that's a nice gesture Mr Merrill, but I wonder . . . '

'Please Daniel. I'm quite weak. Don't fight me.

'I want you to promise that you will live there. It's important for me to know that the house will be lived in by my children . . . by my child. It's a kind of continuity. It's strange how these things can take on such importance when there are no more distractions . . .

'Don't tell lies for them Daniel, promise me that at least. However important you think the struggle is. Once the truth goes, everything goes. A system of law . . . some basis of civility to deal with one another . . . Once it is gone, what's left?

'Don't disparage mercy. I've come to the conclusion that every man whores after his own strange god. Each of us to his own idolatry. And many more of us make human sacrifices than end up in the law courts answering for it.

'My idol I suppose was judgement. I spent too little time on mercy. Faith hope and charity. But the greatest of these is charity. Father forgive them for they know not what they do – that's what Jesus cried out even as the nails went home. A generous judgement, Daniel, a reversal of judgement in fact. A reversal I think we might all end up needing.'

'Do you believe in God then?' Daniel asked, surprised. 'Claire always said that deep down you couldn't believe in anything.'

'The evidence is far from conclusive, though the book upon which both plaintiff and defendant swear is unambiguous: "The fool says in his heart, There is no God." And if I can't fully acknowledge the Lord's existence, I can most readily acknowledge my own folly.'

Alfred Merrill died later that evening. Daniel, who was at his bedside holding his hand, wept.

He arrived back in London exhausted. There was a note from Smart to contact him as a matter of urgency. Then he found out how Claire had absconded from the party in the USSR, and they had returned home without her.

He went back to the house disconsolate and confused. He did not know what to make of it. What had she done? He felt an odd primitive fear rising inside him.

He looked through the newspapers which had piled up during his absence. One photograph halted him. It was Hitler at the party rally in Bückeberg in 1934. Out of the geometric sea of flags and armbands holding the swastika's recurrent crippled gesture, the Führer stepped upwards to the camera's eye, out of the crowd, like a new form of life just emerging.

✦   ✦   ✦

The police were prepared to write it off as another insoluble accident, with suspicious circumstances. They had examined the tyremarks on the road and had come to the conclusion that, given their unusual thickness, a lorry or van must have been using that road late on the night in question. It was unusual but not unthinkable. The chances of locating either vehicle or driver were remote.

It was the telephone call from the landlord of The Boar's Head which re-activated their interest. The more he heard about the rich fellow in the flash car and how he had sped off that night with a fair amount of scotch inside him, the more he brooded about the local couple in their Morris who had crashed to their deaths.

Lindsay Cragge worked in Beaconsfield at the petrol station there. The wife of the landlord at the Boar's Head dropped in to see her the day before the police arrived, and alerted her to her husband's detective work. So when the inspector turned up the following day, he looked at a very different figure from the one Aubrey Innis had seen.

Wearing a plain black dress and flat shoes, Lindsay had plaited her hair so it hung down in two pony tails. She looked ten years younger. She wore no make-up. She spoke quietly and cried as she revealed that the man who had offered to drive her home in his car that evening had in fact driven her back to London against her will and attempted to assault her. Only her vociferous protests had saved the situation. She had forced him to take her back to Gerrard's Cross so that there should be no scandal. Most of all she had feared for her parents' health, for one scintilla of improper behaviour could, she insisted, have killed her father.

Her performance was compelling. The police believed it. Her new employer believed it. So much so that he married her six months later. They did not have full physical relations until their wedding night. She had explained shyly that she had made a vow to herself as a young girl that she would save herself for marriage. She knew it was old-fashioned but that was the way she was. Not like some of them at The Boar's Head she could name . . .

When the police called at the house in Harrington Gardens Aubrey was not there. The butler kept on since his father's death said he had no idea where the young master was. He never did any more. He had left by car the previous morning with no information conveyed regarding his destination or the length of his visit.

Aubrey was in fact in Oxford. Talking to a bemused pair of undergraduates about John Leland.

'Some have turned him into a scoundrel, you see. They have implied that he was a lackey, selling his mind and his soul to keep in with the king. But it's not true, it's not true at all. He is one of the founders of our culture. He saved treasures from the flame and the spider. He travelled up and down the country making sure these things would not disappear forever.

'He was one of the inventors of chorography. That's the intensive examination of a geographical area to find out the truth about its past. They say that chorography ultimately disproved the very legends he believed in so fiercely. But is not that a proof of his integrity?

'They criticise him for his literalism in believing in the matter of Britain, but they don't understand. The imagination is always literal. The literal is the only language it speaks. And it is imaginative facts we are discussing here.

'If his work failed and was not completed, if he went mad for those last long years of his life, that doesn't make him a dishonourable man, does it? Hasn't madness often been the stigmata of those who are most honest of all?

'Let me get you both another drink.'

'No. No thanks. We must be off. We have a tutorial . . . '

Aubrey was left alone again. The landlord was wiping a glass and looking over at him carefully. Aubrey finished his pint and left.

When he arrived back at his car, an observant young constable was standing at the side of it.

'Would you be Aubrey Innis, sir, by any chance?'

When Aubrey saw his lawyer the following day, the picture that was outlined for him was dark but by no means hopeless.

'The driving offence will result I suspect in the loss of your license for a minimum of a year, but I doubt there'll be a custodial sentence.

'This other business is rather more tricky. The girl is claiming indecent assault, and I wouldn't like to judge the mood of a jury on this one. She's only fifteen. Did you know that?'

'How old was Salomé?'

'One remark like that in court and they'll bang you up, sir, make no mistake about it.'

'But I didn't even touch her . . . Well, I touched her, but I didn't have her . . . I mean, she would have done. Damn it. I took her back again.'

'It all looks a bit nasty, Mr Innis. Beware the conscience of the public. You're a wealthy man and she is a fifteen year old girl. From the photograph I saw in the *Watchword* this morning she looks set to enter a convent.'

'The photograph lies.'

'It may do, but its lie may be stronger than your truth.'

Aubrey stood up to leave.

'The man and woman . . . In the car . . . '

Mr Gregory looked down at his papers.

'Yes, a bad business. Young couple.'

'The child?'

'A little boy, I believe. The grandparents are alive, fortunately, so it should not be necessary to place him in an orphanage.'

'I'd like to help. With money, I mean . . . '

'Any gesture of that nature will, I am afraid, immediately be construed as an acknowledgement of responsibility for the deaths . . . You must not do anything of this nature without consulting me first. And you must be very wary of talking to the press, who are I fear about to take a strong interest in this case. But then, forgive me, a man such as yourself does not need to be told about newspapers . . . '

He took her for one last sweet elegiac drive through the Cotswolds. She behaved immaculately as always. He did love that car. Then he put her in the garage and sealed the doors with old cloths he had used to clean her.

That elegant monster of perfection brought into the world by Captain W.O.Bentley growled remorselessly on to the last drop of petrol. Innis' insides, corrupted by two decades of indulgence, were no match for the insides of his car which had been pieced together with much love and little malice, and functioned accordingly.

They found his body slumped in the driver's seat. His insides were smoked as though by internal combustion. They suspected foul play at first because of the handcuffs holding his right hand to the driving wheel. On examination though they let the matter drop. The cuffs were museum material from around the turn of the century. Even more mysteriously, they had been sawn apart at some point, then welded together again. They carried an engraved device along one side: "Houdini. Nothing to lose but your chains. Arthur."

They reasoned that had he been attached by someone else to the car, then there would have been some chafing of his wrist from his attempts to escape the scene. But there was none. No suicide note either.

On his desk was a single sheet of paper. On it was written:

Merlin
Chapter One
Leland's Journey

People mythologise. They tell a lot of fancy lies. They prefer talk to silence. Even the most eloquent silence.

✧   ✧   ✧

Aubrey's obituary appeared in the same copy of the *Daily Watchword* as Alfred Merrill's:

A fine and distinguished journalistic talent, cut tragically short by personal grief.

Bobbie Morrell had written it. She had gone back to the beginning and read all his pieces. She had been astonished at how good he had been before he let it fall away in boredom and dissatisfaction.

She sat in the publisher's office as he read it.

'That's excellent Bobbie. You've seen him off well.'

'He was good. The guy was really good. Did you know that?'

'Nobody ever really knows anything till it's too late.'

'He could have been something important, Arthur.'

'Maybe he was.'

'He was a great journalist. Why couldn't he just accept that? Instead he has to pack it in to go write his asshole Arthurian romance.'

'He's dead Bobbie.'

'I've noticed Arthur.'

She did not want this conversation to end. Too much ended with it. She looked at him and he looked through the window at St Paul's.

'You leave today, I gather.'

'That's right.'

'Lucky goes with you, I understand.'

'Yes. To the house on the Hamble. Lucky will be my . . . personal assistant.'

'Your personal assistant Arthur?'

'That's what I said. You surely don't think they must all be numbered amongst the seraphim? You of all people.'

'It's just those words . . . now.'

She reached out a hand towards his, but his withdrew.

'You might at least say you're fucking sorry Arthur.'

He turned and looked her full in the face, his left eye already going, but the fierceness still there in the expression.

'Does the disease apologise to the victims it must consume?'

Arthur Smithson-Lowe's Rolls-Royce arrived at his country house late that afternoon. Lucky leant him an arm as they made their way into the hall. There a servant bowed and handed the publisher an envelope.

'Open it Lucky' he said.

It was from Camper and Nicholson:

Kaiser is this day completed. And a beautiful boat she is, sir.

CHAPTER FIVE

Brightness Falls:1945

One day in 1945 there fell from the sky a message of the worst that man might do. It dropped according to the laws of gravity, and for a moment its curves caught and reversed the sun's rays. Innocent and swift, it homed to its target. Before it landed (for it never did land) the inhabitants of Hiroshima thought the sun itself had hit them and shattered in a million burning fragments.

Atoms: the best men do by way of explanation. No matter. Men can manipulate what they cannot grasp, this being their strange and terrible grace.

A normal day in Japan. There happens to be a war on, but the old brood still on a vanished past they have invented and the young dream of an unreal future. On this day though they both wake to a greater unreality, for they witness a miracle. The fundaments of matter run amok, coaxed into this anarchy by the patient skill of scientists. Nature's prompted swerve and man's new mastery etches itself on their skin. These are now the children of the sun. Their bright curse must last for many generations.

The fliers whooped at their mission accomplished as they headed back. They left behind them the glare of a new terror, screams loud enough to wake a sleeping god.

✧　　✧　　✧

At 11 o'clock on the morning of August 7th, Helen Dukas heard the White House announcement on the radio. She hurried out into the garden and told Albert Einstein the news.

Oy vay, he said.

He'd helped to persuade Roosevelt to develop the bomb in case the Nazis should get there first. But his implication in this matter was in any case complete. When Lise Meitner split a uranium atom in two pieces in 1939, she gauged the resulting nuclear energy by means of an equation simply formulated as $E = mc^2$.

Call matter energy coaxed into a stable form, energy the potency of that form in movement. The lovely symmetry of these perceptions had once opened the universe up to him, like a rose.

He stayed bent gazing at the ground. He liked the Japanese. On his wretched tours around the globe they were the only ones who did not bustle him about and make him long for anonymity. And when they asked for his autograph, instead of a stubby little pencil and a scrap of crumpled paper, they had offered him a length of silk and a brush dipped in purple ink.

❖   ❖   ❖

Daniel Miskin was glad it was over. He went down into Alfred Merrill's excellent cellar and picked the best claret he recognised. He raised the first glass of it to the picture he had placed on the wall – the one of Adolf Hitler stepping up out of the unknown element of his supporters.

'Stay dead will you' he said and emptied his glass. Then he walked over and took down that picture which he had made himself live with for as long as the world had to live with the reality it portrayed. Then he refilled his glass.

It had not been easy. Keeping the faith had not been easy. Before the war had started so many had gone – Kamenev, Zinoviev, Bukharin – the men he had idolised as a young cadre in the party. He had memorised sentences of these people's work. They were his comrades, however far apart they lived. To hear them denouncing themselves as traitors produced a shiver of distrust through him. But then he had always told Claire, the future would not be easy to gain.

Then there had been the loops they had to jump back and forth through. First there was the non-aggression treaty, which had stunned them into utter confusion. At a special meeting at the headquarters in King Street, they had formulated the phrasing for their new line. A war would be foolhardy. Then Russian troops moved into Poland. Bread taken to the starving Polish peasants, lied the *Daily Worker*. Next the USSR wanted a policy of benevolent neutrality towards the Germans. There was a split in the British Politburo. They ended up by abasing themselves and sending into internal exile the few members who still had some feathers of truth clinging to their shredded garments. The best way to help in the struggle against Hitler, declared the Central Committee, was to fight against Chamberlain and Churchill.

The British, the French and the Polish, they continued, bore as much responsibility as the German Fascists for the war now being fought.

Come the end of November, the USSR invaded Finland. Another liberation, declared the *Daily Worker*. Many left, sickened now beyond loyalty. But Daniel did not leave. He simply stopped going to meetings. He stayed home and read. When in the June of 1941 the Germans invaded Russia, he felt a profound sense of relief. Now for the first time he could support the defeat of Hitler without denying his communism.

Of all the things that Daniel had read during this time, nothing had held him more, nor brought him back more often, than Alfred Merrill's diaries. In the same official leather binding as his law books, they had escaped Daniel's attention for the first two years he'd lived at Stratford Road. One day he lifted one off the shelf out of idle curiosity. After that, it was almost a nightly activity.

He had started with himself and Claire. Once he realised how methodical and scrupulously dated they were, he thought of the relevant times and looked them up. For a little while, he started to hate the man he thought he had come to love. Entries like the following did not help:

> Claire arrives tonight with her communist. A not-unintelligent member of the working-class. A little coarse. Graceless in dress and manner – inevitably I suppose. Claire uses people to make her gestures.

It took a while before he could forgive him that. Or this:

> Claire arrived tonight obviously wishing to stay as short a time as was required to be given her money. It did occur to me not to give it at all. I asked her why her Bolshevik fancy man didn't provide for her. It wouldn't be enough even if he did, she said. At least there's the physical satisfaction to be had, I ventured. Great proletarian lover, you mean, was her reply. No hardly. He's too busy reading Lenin to be much use in that department.

It was with his wife's death that the diaries became truly interesting:

> The ship's purser, a young fellow, had apparently showed her some kindness but was entirely unprepared for her entry into his cabin that night. Horrified by her physical advances, he had repelled her. Then he fretted lest she should come to harm. At three that morning he went off to make sure she was in her cabin. Finding she was not, he raised the alarm.
>   It was damn decent of the captain to hush the business up in this way . . .

At the time when he had discovered his disease would kill him, there was this:

> I have to be frank with myself and admit that I have been a cold unloving man. Even given the odd circumstances in

which I married my wife – her arrival in my rooms that night, the hysterical pregnancy – I could still have served her better than I did. She needed warmth and affection I suppose. She received none from me.

Claire was born from this sorry match. Her coldness is her revenge. Daniel whom I have come to like is her revenge upon us all. God help him with his idiot dialectical nonsense. He colludes in evil. History exonerates them all apparently, marching on relentlessly to the socialist millenium. He is an intelligent and friendly man who has obliterated that part of his brain which would see the horrors of his cause.

What can you do? You listen, feel nauseous at injustices excused, and you smile.

This particular night, in any case, Daniel finished the bottle of red wine and set off, an inch unsteadily, towards the meeting. It was down in Battersea. On the top floor of a pub whose landlord was a member – one of the new ones, one of the many who had joined once they had all started fighting on the same side. Daniel hailed a cab. The arrangements Alfred Merrill had made for him meant that he was not short of money. On the way he thought with mild irritation that he would not be able to eat. Nor would he be able to have any more claret. It was either beer or whisky. He would choose whisky.

He sat, as usual, impassively though the proceedings. Anxieties were expressed about paper sales, about losing the initiative to the Labour Party. If they weren't careful, said one old hand, the forces of reformism could disembowel them.

It was only at the end – he was almost asleep with the wine and the whisky – that the words came from the platform . . . Comrade Merrill's house. Silence suddenly obtained. Eyes turned towards him. He sat up quickly.

'I'm sorry comrade. You'll have to repeat that. My hearing isn't what it was, as you know.'

Harry Smart stood up again. He looked hard at Daniel.

'We were saying comrade that now seems to be an appropriate occasion to discuss the disposal of Comrade Merrill's property.

'Before leaving for her sojourn in the Soviet Union from which she has still not returned, Comrade Merrill told the Party it was to make use of her father's house. That house has since been occupied solely by you comrade.

'Now the situation has obviously been somewhat delicate. Your relationship with Comrade Merrill was not merely of a political nature . . . Well, when she disappeared like that, your feelings were obviously taken into account. But a long time has elapsed since then. None of us know what has happened to Comrade Merrill. Perhaps we never will. She might never come back, how can we know?

'The comrade has, to put it mildly, been something of an embarrassment to most of us here. It was after all on a cordial visit to the Motherland of Socialism that she absconded. Took up with an undesirable in that country, apparently, a counter-revolutionary so-called poet. This is the information we have received.

'Whatever she has done, she has not helped this movement, which she claimed was her life – as it is all our lives of course. As it is yours, comrade.

'Anyway, to return to her father's house. We were given permission by her to use it. That permission has never been revoked. There are some in this branch, comrade, who have been a little surprised that the initiative for all this has not come from you yourself. A large house like that, after all, a memento in brick and lime of the most brutal and triumphalist epoch of the bourgeois ascendancy . . . A communist, one would have thought, might feel a little uncomfortable in it, all alone . . . '

A retch of laughter came from the back of the room.

'Our suggestion comrade' Smart continued, smiling, 'is this. No-one wants you to be homeless, though of course the house on Primrose Hill was of a sort that many of our members could only dream of . . . Why not move your things on to the top floor. The lower floors can then be taken over by the organising committee, the bookshop and the youth section.

'We do hope you will agree to this plan, comrade. We're desperate for space and the Soviet victory could provide us with opportunities as yet unforeseen.'

Smart sat down. Eyes shifted over to Daniel, who realised that he would have to say something, though he had no wish to.

'I'll have to think about it' he said finally.

Smart rose again. His tone this time was vicious.

'Comrade, it is not your place to *think* about it. It is not, if Comrade Merrill was to be believed, your property to dispose of.'

'It is though' Daniel said, rising, and sobered by fury. 'It is mine and hers, but independently mine all the same in her absence.

'Such were the terms of her father's will. Had you been courteous enough comrade to consult me about the use of my house, instead of organising this paltry little putsch, then I would have informed you of these things.

'Claire I see now has become a criminal. I think I'd like to examine the nature of her criminality . . . '

'Comrade, this is hardly the place as you know . . . ' Smart started.

'Why don't you shut up Smart' Daniel said, breaking the code of fraternal debate for the first time in his life. 'Why don't you shut your self-righteous little fucking mouth and listen.

'Comrade Merrill I gather has disgraced herself by associating with an anti-social element in the USSR. A degenerate, according to the official report. Well, I have to tell you, that I rather doubt that. Claire's tastes were erratic, even quirky, but I doubt they stretched as far as the degenerate. And since we've all decided to get so personal and frank, I very much doubt anything could be as degenerate as those gaudy musclemen on posters, wielding their spades, which you have instead of wallpaper in your home, Smart.

'Something has degenerated, it's true. But I don't think it's Comrade Merrill somehow. Kamenev, Zinoviev, Trotsky, Bukharin . . . So many casualties. The very finest they had, so we had thought. Uncle Joe has won the struggle I think, but it has occurred to me for some time he might have lost the revolution.

'I have had the leisure over the last few years to register the fact that a dialectical truth . . . is another word for a lie.'

Daniel stood up. He was tired. He looked about him at expressions of accusation and astonishment.

'This is my family I've lost here Smart' he shouted suddenly.

As he opened the door he heard Smart starting up again.

'Comrades, in my twenty years in the communist movement this is the most blatant example of recidivist . . . '

He woke up the next day hungover.

Beth Trevelyan stood there with her bag in her hand. She had let herself in with the key he had given her. Despite her own misgivings, they had become lovers. I *would* leave her to marry you, he had told her. But how can I leave someone who's disappeared?'

'So?' she said.

'I think I've just left the party.'

'I've read the whole of that bloody book by Lenin and now you've left the party?'

'Sorry.'

'Something more important than that anyway, you randy old bugger' she said slipping out of her clothes to slide in beside him.

'What could be more important?'

'I thought you told me your wound in the war meant you couldn't have any children?'

'That's what they told me.'

'Looks like you should have taken a second opinion, Dan.'

✧   ✧   ✧

When Marianne Morris had been summoned to the reading of

Aubrey Innis' will, she had thought at first that some hideous deception was being practised upon her. After her conversion she had dried out and cleaned herself up. She had a job running a fruit stall in Hammersmith and found the companionship which that afforded greatly to her taste.

She had worn the best clothes she had to the lawyer's office. A kindly solicitor had to explain to her three times that the terms of the will were quite explicit. Half of Aubrey Innis' wealth went to the little boy who had been orphaned the night of the incident on the road from Oxford and the other half, including his house, and his collection of modern art to her.

'Buy why?' she had asked.

' "In recompense" are the only words of explanation used.'

She went to see the house. She realised with a certain amount of fear that she wanted to live there, though some of the more wildly erotic *objets d'art* might have to be removed. She made her way over to Farm Street and waited until she could see Father Tyrrell.

'I don't see what it is you're so anxious about' he said. 'The Lord giveth and the Lord taketh away. Blessed be the name of the Lord.'

'He also says, Blessed are the poor' she replied. 'Perhaps this is a test. Perhaps I should sell all he's left me immediately and give it to the poor . . . '

'Perhaps' he said, 'though if you finish the quotation you started above I think you will find it says, Blessed are the poor for they shall inherit. Now that prediction is usually read eschatologically. But perhaps . . . in your case . . . the eschaton has arrived a little early . . . '

'You're making fun of me' she said.

'That's not very difficult you know, Marianne. There are occasions when you give the impression of having been . . . created for the purpose. Now for goodness sake don't start weeping. How many times have I told your tear time is finished.

'Come on. Let's go and have a look at this pile of bricks you think might imperil your soul.'

They went to the house together. He marvelled at the collection which Innis had brought together. In his own way he must have been very devoted, he said.

'He knew what he was doing, that's for sure' Marianne said.

'Well there you have it then. You have been given back your gallery – the one you lost in 1914. Open it. Call it the Innis Gallery. It can be a home turned into an exhibition, like the John Soane Museum in Lincoln's Inn Fields. You can still keep one part purely for yourself. That's the part you can give me tea in . . . '

He handed her the sachets he had put in his pocket.

'And for all this spiritual direction all I ask is . . . a little cheddar and a crust.'

'Are you fasting?' she had asked.

'We all will be soon.'

So another war had passed Marianne by as she organised the house ready for its opening to the public when peace returned. And as she re-hung and classified and typed out biographical notices, she thought of two men. One was her son whom she had last seen when she slapped him across the face, and the other was Arthur Smithson-Lowe . . .

The celebrations on the streets had already come and gone when Lucky showed up. He had been wounded in Italy and walked with a slight limp. But he looked handsome in his uniform. His father's features had become more pronounced. She hugged and hit him at the same time.

'Not one letter. You could have written one letter, one card. I didn't know where you were, whether you were alive or dead . . . '

'I'm alive mother' he said with a smile 'and extremely hungry.'

They spent the rest of that day together. He explained his war and she explained her inheritance and her belief.

'Was father a catholic?' he asked her.

'Yes of course he was. He'd seen too much of hell to believe anything else.'

'How many of his paintings are here?'

'Three' she said. 'Good ones. I mentioned you in the biographical note underneath them. Now I can finish it off. I was frightened I might have to write, "Killed in the . . . " '

'Well you didn't did you? I've come back, though plenty haven't.'

He smiled at her.

'Early night tonight' he said. 'We've got to be up and off sharpish in the morning.'

'Why? Where are we going?'

'To Hampshire of course. To the house of Arthur Smithson-Lowe.'

When his boat had been completed he had named it Kaiser – to the horror of the sailing fraternity in those parts and his own skipper, Martin. Once fortified by drink, Martin had turned to him and said,

'Mr Smithson-Lowe sir, why did you lumber this beautiful boat with that Kraut moniker?'

Smithson-Lowe looked at the man with some interest.

'In memory of my old friend Friedrich Bechstein. A nice man. Made very good pianos. Built the Bechstein Hall so concerts could be held there. Very good acoustics I gather. But then you've probably heard them. That's the Wigmore Hall now, you see, where the BBC holds its little shindigs. The government took it from him during the war, and they never gave it back. Just because he had, as you would put it, a Kraut moniker.

'As did of course the First Lord of the Admiralty in those days, Louis Battenberg. And as I remember our own dear kings and queens. Now instead of Hanovers we have Windsors. And instead of Battenbergs we have Mountbattens. And this boat Martin will be called Kaiser for as long as I'm alive.'

Soon after, Smithson-Lowe became completely blind. When

war broke out he had black sails fitted and camouflaged the hull. He continued sailing. Every day whatever the weather.

The fierce blindman in his inky waterproofs, staring vainly out to sea while Martin shouted instructions to him which way to turn the wheel and for how far. They had both become expert in this partnership.

Then Martin had been called up and the publisher could find no others prepared to risk their lives and reputation sailing a boat called Kaiser along the English coast with a blind man at the helm. Smithson-Lowe withdrew inside and never ventured out again.

In the unlighted house he would stumble about, knocking things over and cursing. He drank brandy from the bottle. Sometimes he shouted with the pain, but he would do anything to avoid the terrors of sleep – and that dream.

He had told the dream in detail to Dr Merton:

Enormous crabs were pincering their way out of the ocean, an immemorial pilgrimage timed to the same tide and the same day of each year. So it had been since before human life arrived on the planet. Their purpose a cold and driven sex, the reproduction of a world of giant crabs, then back to the watery blank. A sun was fixed above barrenness which allowed for no time passing for there was no means of measurement. And in the dream he sailed in closer and closer to the copulating crabs until a pincer held him down . . . then the scream woke him and he had come to believe that the one time it didn't, he would be dead.

'It's one dream, Merton, and I want it out.'

'Out, Arthur?'

'I want you to kill that dream inside me. It's quite specific. Can you not locate it and . . . expunge it?'

'No.'

'Find a specialist. There must be one presumably. Isn't this the century of psychology, psychiatry . . . opening up the mind of man and putting it right. I thought that fellow Freud was meant to have detected the hidden clockwork of the soul, so now anything could be re-arranged if it proved unworkable.

'There is surely someone in Harley Street who, with a sufficently large fee to encourage him, can isolate one dream and . . . take it out.'

'I fear not Arthur, though I have little doubt there are a number who'd take your money and tell you they could.'

Dr Merton lifted up the brandy bottle.

'Hard liquor and your medication don't mix though. It probably aggravates . . . '

'Bugger off Merton' Smithson-Lowe said with sudden vehemence.

'I'll die as I choose. Just as I lived.'

When they arrived, Lucky stopped and looked at the manicured lawn that sloped down to the water and at Kaiser moored down at the bottom.

'He's dying in style anyway' his mother said as she linked her arm through his.

'Arthur does everything in style' Lucky said.

This was not long before the end and it took some time for the old servant to convey his information to his employer. Finally he understood and pulled himself up by the servant's sleeves.

'Is it Lucky, did you say? Is Lucky here?'

They were brought through into the room. It smelled of medicine and drink and a body moving swiftly to the grave.

He placed his hands on Lucky's face and caressed him. He held his ears and his mouth. He ran his fingers down the sides of his nose and stroked his forehead.

'My my Miss Morris but what a beautiful boy you have. And him made out of wedlock too. Well there must have been some sport back there all those years ago in Montmartre, because he's a child of love if ever there was one.

'But shrewd with it, eh Lucky? The only one of all who came

my way whose mind ran as fast as my own.'

'What about Aubrey Innis?' asked the curator of the Innis Gallery.

'No, Aubrey's trouble was he believed in redemption. But he just didn't know where to find it. You don't believe in redemption though, do you Lucky?'

'No' he said.

'That's my boy. That's my beautiful boy. But you've been off fighting to save democracy. How was that?'

'Engaging.'

'Wounded?'

'In the leg. Nothing too serious.'

'Did you . . . did you believe in it?'

'In staying alive yes. Just as you do now Arthur, though the odds are stacked so heavily against you.'

'You will stay for dinner, of course. This lump of rotting flesh can be bathed and dressed. You'd be surprised . . . You will stay . . . please.'

It was a word neither of them had ever heard Arthur Smithson-Lowe use before. They stayed. Sure enough, when Arthur was led into the dining room he looked splendid. He had been cleaned up and was immaculately dressed. They were served a five course meal.

'You must be hungry after the war, Lucky.'

'Yes Arthur. I did miss your hospitality once or twice.'

'Rationing does not appear to have greatly affected you Arthur' Marianne said quietly.

'Well, I've been saving my coupons you know . . . And these wines were mine to start with. I would have gladly given the whole cellar for the war effort if asked, but they wouldn't appreciate it you know. I once tried it years ago and . . . they don't thank you, frankly.

'You are opening the Innis Gallery I believe Marianne.'

'Next month' she said.

'So Aubrey did find a place amongst the moderns, after all.'

They went back to London the next day. And the following week Lucky returned to camp. Each weekend thereafter Marianne Morris locked up the museum where she lived and made the journey to Hampshire. Smithson-Lowe registered neither pleasure nor surprise. But on the fourth weekend, his car was waiting outside her door to take her with less inconvenience to his home.

It was less than a month after that, the end came. She was prepared. She had placed the little crucifix at the foot of his bed and the Russian icon of the virgin on the table beside him. Being blind he could not complain.

'What did that old fraud Merton tell you out there?' he asked.

'Oh well the usual . . . '

'Don't lie to me Marianne.'

'He said you'll never see morning Arthur.'

'I haven't seen morning for a long time. Put that bottle in my hands, that's a good girl.'

'He also said you mustn't . . . '

'What difference can it make now?'

She handed him the bottle and he poured as much of it as he could get down his throat.

'Have one yourself Marianne.'

Marianne had sworn off drink since the day of her conversion. But she had a glass of water to hand. She chinked her glass against his bottle.

'I have one Arthur. I'll forget my temperance vows just this once.'

'It's just like old times' he said. 'We could be in Paris again Marianne. You could be telling me I'm a good man really. You did once say that, didn't you?'

'Twice Arthur.'

'Well you've learnt you were wrong about that one anyway.'

'I've learnt a lot of things Arthur. I don't expect people to be good anymore. The good has to come along and save them despite themselves.'

'That sounds like redemption talk to me.'

'Perhaps all talk is redemption talk when it finds its proper subject.'

'We don't believe in redemption, your son and I.'

'I'll have time to work on him later. But there is redemption Arthur. There is a force of love . . . '

'No' he groaned, 'don't do this to me now.' He took another pull of the bottle and his face started to turn blue as he swallowed it.

'I'd never have let you in if I'd known you wanted to trap me into this. If someone did set us in motion then he's malevolent. He has an ugly sense of humour. He gives us these carcasses to live in with bits that go hard so we have to stick them into other people. We pay other people to let us stick them in, or get them stuck into us. Then the spirochaete eats us up and steals our sight.

'Maybe it's a Nazi god that kills its own children. He's certainly got a nose for a good sacrifice, this God of yours.

'We all need someone to test our evil on' he said, after a pause and in evident pain. 'Someone to cleanse the miserable claptrap of our charities.'

'Someone to crucify' said Marianne.

She was kneeling at his bedside when he let out the final cry. Speaking quietly she asked him to let her do the praying for him. All he had to do was assent to the words. She told him she was placing in his hands something they might once both have agreed was a sacred object. He took it and he held it tightly.

The publisher died at five that morning and went to whatever heaven, hell or oblivion awaited him.

In the morning the servants refused to push back the sheets from the corpse because of the strange shape sticking up under the sheets over the dead man's chest. With a kind of superstitious fear of all last things, they thought it might be some weird and cancerous growth with a posthumous life of its own. When Doctor Merton pulled back the bedclothes he found that

Smithson-Lowe's hands were clenched around the sculpted figure of a dancer. The figure could have been either male or female. The extraordinary delicacy of its epicene limbs made it an object of much admiration for some time to come. It was even rumoured that the newsman was secretly a brilliant artist, and that great quantities of his work were concealed about the house.

When the estate was auctioned off, the work was identified as that of Henri Gaudier-Brzeska, the young artist who had died in the Great War. No-one was ever to discover how Smithson-Lowe had come by it. But Marianne Morris made sure it ended up in the Innis Gallery.

❖ ❖ ❖

A week before Nathan Corinth was released from prison, he was visited by a fellow countryman of his, Colonel Tom Maitland.

Nathan had spent the years prior to the war writing increasingly fierce articles for magazines like Sir Oswald Mosely's *Action*. He had said that any Briton who went to war against Hitler or Mussolini was a traitor to his country. He had also said that if the Germans wanted to be rid of Jews who'd run the money racket of a rotten civilization, that was their business.

They'd arrested him under the emergency powers in May of 1940. He was in Brixton originally. Then they transferred him a year later to Peel Camp on the Isle of Man. A.D.Carvely had written letters to see if it might be possible to have him released. He is after all, he wrote, one of the undoubtedly great writers of our times, though with famously foolish political views. But then he had conducted an interview with Corinth in prison. Afterwards he said to one of his colleagues, Nathan's safer left where he is until the war is over. If we get him out, someone will surely kill him.

Sexual frustration was his greatest problem. The food and sleeping conditions were no worse than he had been used to in many other places. He was with relatively cultivated individuals, as prison company goes. And he improved his German. He also wrote *Medea Five*. Having no books at all to consult except those he hated, he found those things inside himself he had shored against the age's ruins.

The young colonel who arrived to see him had admired him enormously while at school before the war. At Harvard before joining the army he had been completing his doctoral dissertation, *The Fractured Vessel: Modernity and the Poet* and a great deal of what he had written was addressed to Corinth's work. Now he was back from Germany, liaising with British Intelligence on the Rat Line, and he had made it his business to discover the poet's whereabouts. He was determined to see him. War had reduced them to two Americans on allied soil – one a poet, the other a soldier.

He had in his briefcase the photographs – some already published in the papers, some not – taken of the death camps as the Allied troops entered them.

Nathan was confused at first by the visit. He thought he was to be interrogated again, though no-one in any position of authority had ever dreamt he had information worth acquiring. He was simply a public liability, an embarrassment.

'First, courtesy dictates I register my admiration for your work' the colonel said. 'I have read it since I was sixteen. The sheer power of your language and your imagery seems to me to be unsurpassed.

'It was because of that great admiration that it pained me so much when you saw fit to align yourself with the fascist powers immediately before the war and – from what I hear – throughout it. I've been told on good authority that at any time during the hostilities you could have been released had you indicated that you now supported the Allies in their struggle . . . '

Nathan was rubbing his cheek vigorously with one hand. His gaze switched from the table to the door and then the window but avoided the colonel's eyes.

'I wanted to show you these because the first thing I ever

learned from you, in your introduction to *Medea One*, was that a writer takes responsibility for his words. They are his weapons and his creatures you said. He is obliged to see they should correspond to both justice and reality.'

He laid out the photographs across the desk.

'They are mostly of Auschwitz' he said. 'And these people are mostly Jews, though plenty of others died in them. Gypsies, socialists, trade unionists, those of an exotic sexual disposition . . . This is what happened at the end of the words.'

Nathan's eyes swung from the window to the door to the face of the young colonel at last, then down onto the photographs. He lifted up one after another. Mountains of bones and skulls. Figures shrunk to nothing but pain, skin and pain, their huge eyes beseeching from their bunks. Beseeching whom? Beseeching what? He started to mumble as he shuffled the pictures, one after another.

'The Greeks had no sense of sin you know. Life manifests its powers. Sometimes in this form, sometimes that. If you try to find their religion – their real religion, not the iconic paraphernalia of the gods, you'll find it's this: We are wounded and killed so that songs can be made by our laughing children. The gods do smile occasionally as well as shouting and killing. And when they smile a genius is fashioned down among the crush of faces. Such a one has only a single moral obligation: fulfilment of itself at any cost. Darwin you see was either a liar or a fool. Lamarck is closer to the truth.

'Intelligence and form. Creation consists of these two. These are the signatures of the sacred all about us. And all who lessen the power of the one or the shape of the other are traitors. Whether evolutionary, revolutionary or the simple liberal paraplegic. Intelligence and form. The one the force, the other the experimental shapes surviving the quotidian, the flux.

'Deep in the heart of Demos is self-hate. And a house divided against itself cannot stand. Jesus said that, you know. The Jew Jesus.

Was Jesus humble or did he
Give any proofs of humility?'

The colonel had taken out a typed sheet. He held it in front of him as he spoke.

'They had apparently tried shooting. Too slow. There was a pest-control firm known as Degesch. Produced a potent substance called Zyklon-B. They tried it out first on five hundred Soviet POW's. They were obviously impressed.

'Auschwitz itself was described by one of their own as this greatest of institutions for human annihilation. The orderlies who dropped the crystals of Zyklon-B down their shafts noted they were amethyst blue. Mary's colour you called it in *Medea Two*. Remember?

'The metal columns inside the rooms themselves where the men, women and many many children came were perforated so they could breathe out the poison. Their cries would have been terrible of course but we gather . . . '

'Medusa's macaronic ganglia' Nathan said hurriedly, 'these are the age's conduits. Cut off already, severed from the source of their sustenance. They clamour back you see with a type of fierce nostalgia for the time before Perseus arrived with his blade of choice. That's the sever of truth . . .

'All centuries have had their sacraments. All energy comes from what some call divine and some demonic. And the sacrament of our age is slaughter. We made the sacred itself obscene. The things made holy are the things reviled.

'We have broken Medea's heart. We have snapped the atom, we have broken her. We have done what Jason could not. At the centre of it the temperature was four times greater than in the centre of the sun. We have found the form of creation and broken it. Now Medea has the strength left only to destroy her children. Creon's daughter took the gown and the diadem. They burnt her up. Scorched the flesh off her bones. Charred her to dead fire as the bride bells started ringing. And Creon too, trying to raise up his lovely girl from the dead. The poison cleaned him to a stump. The old and the young a pile of ash.

'She was a prophetess, you must understand. She spoke the future then she killed it, disowning the flesh it had become. Perhaps you are one of them, one of her children, sent with invisible poison to destroy the city?'

The colonel stood up to leave.

'I'll leave those photographs with you.'

He stopped at the door and walked back to the table. He opened his brief case and took out of it *Medea One*. He opened it at the title page, turned it round towards Nathan Corinth and put the pen in his hand. Nathan signed automatically.

'You're the greatest poet I'll ever meet' the young man said and left.

CHAPTER SIX

Illuminations: 1956

This is 1956 so Einstein must have died the year before, leaving his traces behind him.

He reiterated up to the end that the Old One does not throw dice. He never ceased in his massive effort to establish a unified field theory, which would have combined gravitational, electromagnetic and nuclear forces in a single theory of immense beauty. This would have shown the heart of nature, the heart of motion, the heart of attraction and repulsion, the heart of the atom. He said often that he wished everything to be made as simple as possible. But no simpler.

He wanted so desperately to disprove the quantum physics that held sway in the academies. The universe, he knew, had an ultimate coherence to it, it was not conducted like a game of chance. There was a logic, down to the minutest detail, to the architecture of the place he found himself inhabiting. He knew this but could not prove it. He did not prove it during his lifetime, and it has remained unproven after his death.

Quantum physics only establishes the behaviour of atoms in swarms. As a crowd they can be monitored and channelled in this direction or that. But the dignity of logic is denied the individual electron. The great physicist fought for it and lost. When his own atoms recomposed themselves, following incineration, they did so carrying the definitions of a feckless and volatile mob. As such, they were disowned and disinherited by their chief biographer.

Daniel Miskin could never come to terms with Einstein. Despite his great devotion to science, Daniel's instincts told him to stay with Newton. In this he agreed with some of the early

Soviet scientists: the moral warp of capitalism, they said, reflected itself in a scientific world picture from which absolute veracity had been extracted. Daniel loved the Newtonian world of cause and effect. He loved solidity and consequence. He did not want his light to be ambiguous . . .

Light, as they so casually say, was thrown on the subject of Stalin's crimes by Kruschev in his speech to the XXth Party Congress. Something called the cult of personality was denounced. Light too was thrown on the nature of the USSR's fraternal relations with its satellites by the crushing of the uprising in Hungary. And light was thrown on how far Britain had ceased to be an empire by its slipshod and deceitful intervention in the Suez Crisis.

Daniel Miskin read the papers and shook his dignified white head.

'I'd best keep Freddie out, I suppose' Beth said.

'Let him come in at the end' Daniel replied. 'We might both need him by then.'

At two o'clock the man arrived with the BBC crew. He was younger than Daniel had expected. Very proper too and businesslike. From some university, but Daniel could not remember the name. Since his book had appeared there seemed to be an army of them, turning up to squeeze the history out of him.

The interview halted and rambled. It seesawed and limped. Daniel had in any case started to meander somewhat in his conversation. He rambled on about Orage and Gurdjieff, figures who had come to occupy his imagination more and more of late.

'I wandered into the graveyard at Hampstead Parish Church the other day. Orage is buried there. On his tombstone there's an enneagram chiselled by, of all people, Eric Gill. A circle divided into nine parts. Gurdjieff claimed it explained everything, as far as I can see . . . I'll be honest, I can make neither head nor tail of it. Can't really even be bothered trying.

'But it did set me thinking that we couldn't live inside those theories. They were barely habitable by the mind of man. Our dialectical materialism, our scientific disregard for everything but something we called progress. That's why Orage crashed through the barrier to the other side. But then that side wasn't habitable either.

'All the scientists were in search of mysticism and all the mystics wanted to be scientific. I personally think that Gurdjieff was a bully, a charlatan of some brilliance – but apart from Alfred Merrill, Orage was the single most brilliant human being I ever met, and he believed in him. Though not at the end of course . . .

'He said you had to forget the last two centuries, forget everything you'd ever learnt. Trust him alone . . . but you can't do that , you know. You can't dismantle people like that, you have to build on their strengths. That's part of the mistake we made . . .

'I suppose they must have all seen something in him which emanated power. Something exotic – from another time almost. And they all wanted to share that power. He made them think they could. So he taught them some of the hocus pocus he'd learnt – but that wasn't really the source of his power . . . He used his power to control them – Orage came to understand that. But he devoted the central years of his life to this man. Became his promotion agent, effectively. And it probably put him in his grave before his time. Trying to find out where the power comes from.'

'And where does it come from, Mr Miskin?' the young lecturer asked.

'The wrong quarters usually. And goes back there too, crawling along with its loot. If my study of history's taught me anything, it's that.'

The young man was growing bored with this old man's blather and worried that he had no material he could use.

'Your study of history has presumably also shown you that you have given a great portion of your life to the support of tyranny.'

'Say that again' Daniel said slowly.

145

'Your leaving of the party when you did . . . '

'I never really left the party, I just stopped going to it . . . '

'All the same, you have acknowledged the evils perpetrated under the name of communism in your articles in the press.'

'Young man, I have acknowledged what I have acknowledged. But I can't help feeling you are attempting to simplify something which is as complex as the disagreements between men, as complex as the structures of our bodies . . .

'I fought for socialism. Gave my life to it. I'm not ashamed of that, which you seem to be implying I should be. I was born into a society where to be working class was to be precluded from half of what a human being needs. We were told to watch them at the top, enjoying the fruits of existence. And to keep digging the coal, smelting the steel, turning the loom. And to shut up. To know your place. I never accepted that. I didn't accept it then and I don't accept it now.

'History is struggle. It always has been. The hard thing is knowing who to believe. That's the big mistake we made. We wanted to believe so badly that when it should have long been evident that Stalin was a liar and a traitor and . . . yes, a tyrant, we couldn't bring ourselves to believe that because that would have been the end of our future. And the past remember still had some of our comrades locked in its prisons . . . '

'So you would still recommend revolution, then?' the young man said, his hostility growing more apparent.

'Revolution's not something you recommend lad. It's something you inaugurate and endure . . . like a medical operation.'

Young Freddie had wandered into the room and picked up the last words of the conversation. He walked over to the sofa where Daniel was sitting. The sound recordist noted the odd and somewhat delightful rhyme between the old fellow's features and their miniature reflection in his young son.

'What's revolution, dad?'

Daniel smiled down at his child as his face relaxed for the first time.

'It's something that goes round, love, and then brings you back to where you started.'

'Like a wheel' Freddie said.

'Very like a wheel' his father replied.

'You've already cut have you?' the interviewer said somewhat wearily to the sound recordist.

'No' came the reply, 'I thought that was about the best bit, to be honest.'

❖   ❖   ❖

Clara sat on the outskirts of Petersburg. The apartment was full, for many knew of her. The stories abounded. Some said that she was Stalin's secret daughter, a lovechild raised in Switzerland. This, they said, accounted for her strange-sounding Russian. Some said that she was the missing tsarina, the one their bullets bypassed. Those who knew though said she was Litvinov's companion, wife possibly, she would not say. He had disappeared into the gulag. She had spent one month beneath the Lubyanka and then eight years in Siberia, the usual penalty for a member of the family of a traitor to the fatherland.

Some said she was French, some Italian, some English. In any case she spoke nothing but Russian now. And she had learnt every poem Litvinov had ever written by heart.

She prefaced her recitation this day by saying,

'Whatever they tell you, don't believe them. They are the same men who screamed bitch at me in the Lubyanka. When the systems change, they stay in place. Give them the power, they will wipe out the whole world rather than lose their place in it. Don't believe them. Don't ever trust them. Don't ever smile at them.

'I learned Litvinov's verse because it was the only way of making sure they couldn't destroy it. Now I will give back to you what he gave me.'

She spoke with eyes closed, rocking on her seat, for an hour.

His verses lived again on her tongue. She ended with one short one, not his best, but it always reminded her of the night they took him:

To Osip Lost In Exile

It was a time of blizzards over transit camps
　　When the age screwed tight its eyes
Raw from rubbing away the light. A time of
　　Villages with disappearing names
Scattered like salt in the north. Wolf years
　　Behind whose grin lay nothing
But the scorched earth of amnesia. A hunger
　　Cold enough to eat the wind.
So this Dante once more paced the metre of his exile
　　As Guelph and Ghibelline
Between them divided the days. In Voronezh
　　His teeth crunched the bread's
Forgiving snow and, as the crust was torn,
　　His emblematic tongue gave
Benediction. But night intruded and prevailed:
　　A black hood gathered gently
Over the axeman's eyes. Night, that ransacked
　　The apartment, turning up
Those beautiful equations discrediting paradise -
　　Catalogued and packed away in boxes
They were shifted to the centre of the zone.
　　There the temperature was zero,
The population nil, and famished verses drifted
　　Over squares so dead
Euclid would have wept. There an iron lung
　　Hushed with grey breath
The calendar's progress. A spider manoeuvred
　　Round her frail necropolis.
Into the gauze mesh of her eye, stars disappeared

As the weather told lies
To blindfold icons razored out of mute cathedrals . . .

Frosted acres out of which a spadeful of glistening
   Black earth protested.
A solid lake of milk on which a raven landed.
Vladivostok. December. 1938.

When she had finished reciting, she opened her eyes and stared at them all. She stood up then and went back to her bedroom. She did not come out again until they had all left and the place was in darkness.

✧   ✧   ✧

It was almost closing time and Miss Marianne Morris was moving from room to room making sure the visitors had left. In the ground floor gallery there was a young woman of twenty. She was standing in front of the Rovidas taking notes. Miss Morris did not interrupt her. Only when she was finished did the American tourist register her presence.

'Oh, I'm sorry' she said, 'I'm keeping you all behind.'

'You can't keep us behind' Marianne said amiably. 'We live here. Come upstairs.'

Gael Norton followed the kind old lady up the stairs. In the administration area, Lucky was quietly working.

'This is my son, Lucio . . . or Lucky as he prefers to be known. He runs this museum with me. This young lady was making notes in front of the Rovidas . . . '

'Ah' Lucky said 'is he an interest of yours?'

'I'm writing an essay on him for college. My professor thinks that he represents the decisive turning-point.'

'Which one?'

'Oh, between the old world and the new, the traditional and the modern, the harmonious and the fractured.'

149

'Your professor might have something there ' Marianne said, 'though Rovida was hardly alone on that particular cusp. By the way, Lucky is Rovida's son.'

'And she is my mother' Lucky said, and they both laughed.

'You're kidding me aren't you?' the student asked.

'Indeed we are not.'

'Then you must have been Rovida's wife?'

Marianne looked over to the window.

'No . . . not exactly.'

'The passionate engagement between my mother and my father never had any holy water sprinkled upon it.'

'Thank you Lucky.'

'Not even to asperse the troubled parts' he added brightly.

'Thank you Lucky. Thank you now.'

'But you must know so much about him' the student said.

'We probably know as much about him as anyone does. But that's not necessarily a lot.'

'His images seem so tortured . . . so violent. Was he like that?'

'No' said Marianne. 'Or at least, only to himself.'

'My professor wrote an article in which he said that when our twentieth century smiles fade, the terror that lies underneath them is a Rovida canvas.'

'Interesting fellow, your professor' said Marianne. 'Does he paint himself?'

'I don't believe so.'

'Does he actually . . . *like* Rovida?'

'I never asked him. I think he prefers the Renaissance really. But there was no vacancy.'

'Ah, then he is a distant relative of Mr Hake of Illinois.'

'A critic?'

'They all are, believe me. Particularly the ones with the money.'

The student took in, with one last sweep of her eyes, the Rovidas, the Modiglianis, the Picassos and Matisses, and both Lucky and Marianne.

'My professor's annoyed we know so little of his life. He calls him the one who disappeared.'

'Well you tell your professor from me that Rovida's biography would tell him nothing – absolutely nothing – about his art. Wherever he found it, it wasn't in his life. He kept that purely for *self*-destruction.'

'Why did so many of them destroy themselves?'

'I don't know' Marianne Morris said. She walked over to the window and picked up the little Gaudier figure of the epicene bronze dancer. She stood – as she often did – distractedly caressing it as though it were a tiny living creature.

'The gentleman whose name this gallery holds – Aubrey Innis – committed suicide . . . I met him once you know. A most charming young man. But that was a long time ago. One night before the war.'

'You'd better tell her which war, mother' Lucky said without looking up.

'Yes, I always forget that. But there do seem to have been so many . . . '

✧   ✧   ✧

Nathan Corinth sat in the glass conservatory of Shoreman House and waited for his guest to arrive. Mrs Frinton brought him tea and he stared out over the Brighton waves in the cold English sunlight.

'He'll be here soon enough, I'm sure' she said.

'Your company is enough for me, as you know Sal. God, it must have grieved that husband of yours when he left you behind in this world, knowing the men who'd be after you.'

Mrs Frinton smiled and gently smoothed his hair. She had nursed him after his breakdown and then it had seemed natural enough that he simply stay. They had never discussed it.

Ten minutes later Tom Maitland's car pulled into the drive. He climbed out and waved to Nathan as he pulled his briefcase from the passenger seat.

'It's called *Poets in the Age of Destruction*' he said as he showed him the typescript.

'And I'm in it am I?' Nathan asked.

'You are it.'

The poet smiled.

'Does your swanky university pay you enough to take me to lunch?'

'It does. I have been allocated expenses for that very task.'

'And wine?'

'Wine too.'

'Then on this day both Dionysus and Apollo are reconciled. No conflict in the heavens. And look, Tom, it's azure.'

'Mary's colour.'

They ate at the Starfish Restaurant. Nathan gave minute instructions regarding the preparation of his calamary and his trout. He chose the most expensive white wine on the menu.

'You're my only excitement you know Tony.'

'I doubt that Nathan. I doubt it very much.'

'Well there are the ladies of course. Though at my age one must start to take a little care. It's why I avoided the oysters.'

Tom took from his pocket the photograph of his wife and little daughter back in the States and handed it to the poet. He looked at it carefully then gave it back.

'You have a fine family. There'll be more?'

Tom shrugged cheerfully and Nathan raised his glass.

'Multo bambini, eh?'

'I hope so Nathan. You never yourself . . . '

'Too many beds. Too many women. Too many cities. Too many causes.'

'I think you might have made a good father. It might have kept you sane.'

'You've come to the conclusion I was actually mad have you?'

'Yes. Like Merlin, as one of my students wrote, who tried to exercise his power over too large a kingdom when it was falling apart. *Merlinus insanus effectus est*, he entitled his essay on you.'

'He entitled it that did he?'

'He did.'

'Clever little bastard. I hope you marked him down Tom.' Tom Maitland had taken the typescript from his bag.

'Could I read you a little of it Nathan? It is one of the passages you might find most offensive.'

'Then read that one in particular.'

> *During these years Corinth's style became wilder, his pronouncements more and more unpredictable. His obsession with the financial rottenness of western civilization, his awareness of the corruptions in public life, seemed to destroy the powers of judgement in him. So that when the unspeakable evil that Nazism represented was placed before him by history, he was unable to judge it for what it was. He had clamoured so loudly for a solution, that now he could only speak in absolutes. His hatred of the shaggy creature he called Demos was so profound that he could not grasp that he was now supporting the institution of something infinitely more terrible and destructive.*
>
> *His posturing and obscene antisemitism from these years is indicative of the balance he had once held and now lost.*
>
> *The Jewish writers who were and still are his friends testify that he never personally . . .*

'No take that out' Nathan said.

''But I've interviewed Harovitz, I've interviewed Davies . . . '

'I don't care who you've interviewed Tom. Take it out. You are indicting me. So indict me. With complete justice. Don't say I waved them on towards the ovens but was always a good chap to the Jews in my circle. That's what you're saying and it's disgusting.

'Tell the truth. I've taught you that much. And the truth about the others, too. They smiled in self-righteous print while twenty million went to their deaths. All in the name of the harmonious socialistic fellowship of man . . . '

He was silent for a moment, then he turned a startled look towards his companion.

'Do you really believe my words could have taken the flesh from their bones?'

They walked for a while along the promenade together. When they came back into the nursing home, Mrs Frinton greeted them:

'A productive lunch gentlemen?'

'Very much so' Nathan said. 'Young Tom here explained to me how I'd been round the bend for most of the thirties and half of the forties. But he reckons I've improved beyond measure in the fifties.'

'Well I'm glad to hear it' she replied. 'I'll go and make some tea.'

Nathan went and sat in his chair in the corner of the conservatory where he could look at the sea. After a few moments he said:

'You believe in America don't you Tom? You really believe in the good old US of A?'

'I believe I do,' the younger man said happily.

'And with your job at the end of the war you must have known the 761st Tank Battalion presumably?'

'The Black Panthers, yes.'

'I gather Franklin D. put them together as a showcase – originally, that is.'

'I wouldn't know Nathan' Tom said uneasily.

'They were at the liberation of Buchenwald, I'm told.'

'They were indeed – a proud moment for American democracy.'

There was a pause before Corinth spoke again.

'Bit of a shame that when they got back to the home of the brave and the land of the free they had to be shipped around in trains with the blinds down. So I'm told. Lest their white fellow citizens should empty their barrels in those heroes' direction. Uppity niggers I gather still get a rough ride.'

'Nathan, I hope you're not suggesting some equivalence . . . '

'I'm not an equivalence man Tom, you should at least know that by now. I've had almost every sin laid at my feet and have acknowledged the brats as my own, but suggesting equivalences I leave to others.

'I suspect all the same that one or two of those Negroes know of a relative – maybe not so far back in time – who felt the noose slipping over his neck and looked round at the screaming white faces . . . I think they might have told you something about equivalence . . .

'I saw the Movietone, down the road at the local cinema, of the McCarthy hearings . . . what were they called? House of UnAmerican . . . '

'House of Representatives' Un-American Activities Committee.'

'Ah yes, of course. Such a felicitous phrase. How could it have slipped from my mind? The senator didn't look too full of the milk of human kindness to me. I doubt the average commie left to his tender mercies would have come out of it much better than if he'd been visited by Herr Himmler . . . '

'That was an unfortunate episode – he's gone now. I always opposed the campaign.'

'But you are a liberal Tom, n'est-ce pas?'

'I suppose.'

'Never could quite fathom what a liberal believes at all, you know. He seems to believe something midway between the fellow to his left and the fellow to his right . . . '

'We don't believe in slaughtering the innocent anyway Nathan.'

The old poet turned his eyes from the waves and fixed them on Tom. There was still a mesmeric penetration to their blue sharpness.

'And when they laced Dresden with bombs for nights on end until the city was the centre of a fireball, do you think they instructed the flames to leave the innocent untouched? Do you think they marked their lintels for a passover? When Hiroshima went up, when Nagasaki went up . . . '

'We were fighting a war Nathan – against incalculable evil.'

Nathan Corinth turned his eyes back to the swelling and sifting of the Channel. In a much quieter voice he said:

'There you see Tom. You do believe in the slaughter of the innocent. The only difference is, you believe you were right. I no longer believe I was. You can have no conception what that means.

'We had no interest in morality, you know. None. It was sanctity or nothing. And for us, genius was the sanctity of the imagination. We were all with Nietzsche there – beyond good and evil. We left morality the way Gulliver left Lilliput – that was a land for little men. That's why Medea became the centre of it . . . '

'But who is she really Nathan? My students ask me this and I'm often a little vague when I answer.'

'Never be vague. She's what we betray, though I didn't understand that at the beginning. She may be the atom's mystery, probed to the sanctum no man may enter. Jason remember was scientist to his own convenience . . . they haven't nailed the quantum yet though, have they? The hare's still running.

'She was from Colchis – from a barbarous shore. She is magic surrounded on all sides by the city's prose . . . And history too. She's history. She's there in Herodotus, and he *invented* history. Why do you think Euripedes abandoned his beloved polis? He was so sick of its ravaging of everything outside itself. That most rational of men gave us the sound of Medea's scream.

'Did I ever tell you I was there in Paris at the first performance of *Le Sacre du Printemps*? The one they smashed up. I realised then that all we'd ever get to hear of the classical would be its departure. We hear the women keening. The sound of the screams – that's what we harmonise. Pentheus torn apart by women, Oedipus gouging his eyes out so he could no longer see the horror fate had tricked him into – and Medea screaming not at Jason but at a world where Jason flourishes. Who stole her magic then betrayed her so he could get promoted in the city.

'We hear the screams I think but no longer the silence that sustained them. Or what held the silence itself in place: sheer terror. The terror of the gods that no-one could ever question for long. Well, we replaced the terror of the gods with the terror of the state. Starting with Robespierre. And that's when we all started dying by inches.

'Believe me, we live in the age that consumes its children. From the left. From the right. Even, my friend, from somewhere in the middle.'

'And poetry?' Tom asked.

'Poetry's the truth we're left to breathe when the air is poisoned. It's the words the slaughter didn't finish and the moneymen didn't buy, and the politicians didn't bribe, and the newspapers didn't souse with the stain of their bonhomie. It's language hosed free of cant. It's what rinses the attentive mind. It baptises us in the realm of intelligence and form.

'That's what poetry is – and why there's not much of it about.'

'Any here?' Tom asked with a rather bleak smile.

Nathan pulled out from down the side of his armchair a slim typescript.

'*Medea VI?*'

'No. This is the last one. It has a new name.'

He handed it to Tom who read on the title-page *Medea's Children*.

'There were only two, remember' Nathan said, looking out towards the sea again.

'And they both died as I recall' Tom said.

'Truth's blade is sharp.'

'Sign it for me Nathan.'

The old man signed the typescript with a vigorous flourish and they both fell silent. Then Mrs Frinton returned with the tea service. Nathan had put the top back on his pen and was slicing the air with it as though it were an abbreviated sword. As she bent before him to lay out the cups, the poet swung down his pen with great skill to the hem of her skirt and used it to raise the pleated cloth until it was some inches above her knee. It was only then she noticed.

'NATHAN! Really! At your age and with young Tom here too.'

She left the room but it struck Tom that the cause of the pink flush in her cheeks was not necessarily entirely displeasure or embarrassment. He looked carefully into the poet's face. Nathan Corinth gave him a large theatrical wink, and whispered loudly:

'She's weakening.'